"But you, Bethany, are of a different mettle."

A note of deep satisfaction throbbed in his voice. "You will bear me a son."

The shock waves kept rolling through Bethany's mind . . . Zakr wanted *her* to bear his son! She had wanted proof that he did not regard her lightly, but this . . . this was the most serious, far-reaching claim he could possibly make on her. She was horrified by the cold-blooded calculation behind his seduction.

"You don't care what I feel. Or what happens to me," she said in a harshly driven voice.

She heard him sigh, and when he lifted his head his eyes met the turbulent accusation in hers with a haunting need. "On the contrary, I will take the greatest possible care of you."

EMMA DARCY nearly became an actress until her fiancé declared he preferred to attend the theater *with* her. She became a wife and mother. Later she took up oil painting—unsuccessfully, she remarks. Then, she tried architecture, designing the family home in New South Wales. Next came romance writing—"the hardest and most challenging of all the activities," she confesses.

Books by Emma Darcy

EMMA DARCY

the falcon's mistress

Harlequin Books

TORONTO • NEW YORK • LONDON
AMSTERDAM • PARIS • SYDNEY • HAMBURG
STOCKHOLM • ATHENS • TOKYO • MILAN

Harlequin Presents first edition January 1990
ISBN 0-373-11232-7

Original hardcover edition published in 1988
by Mills & Boon Limited

CHAPTER ONE

'MISSING: PRESUMED DEAD.'

Bethany stared at the printed words, and mutiny rose in her heart. She was not going to believe them this time. She didn't care how long her father had been missing. He was not dead. No way. When it came to surviving, Douglas McGregor was the world's best. Hadn't he told her so himself after he was missing and presumed dead in the mountainous jungles of New Guinea?

But Bethany had to allow that surviving in an Arabian desert might present more problems than a tropical jungle. Water and food would not be plentiful for a start; and if her father was separated from his supply of malaria tablets... Something had to be done!

Officialdom had obviously given up on him. After all, an anthropologist who persisted in living with primitive tribes did so at his own risk, and the Australian Government was not about to send a search party into an Arab State for the sake of one eccentric scholar. No one was going to pursue the matter any further. Not actively.

Which only left herself!

And there was no time to waste!

Bethany looked up at the police sergeant who sat rather ponderously in the armchair opposite her. He wore the uneasy expression of one performing

5

a distasteful but unavoidable task. She gave him a sympathetic grimace and rose to her feet.

'Thank you for coming, Sergeant. You've been very kind.'

He quickly pushed himself out of the chair. 'Not at all, Miss McGregor. I regret that...' His hand gestured apologetic helplessness, but his eyes were puzzled as he took in her brisk air of purpose.

He reasoned to himself that she was a nurse—a sister at St Vincent's Hospital—which might account for her calm reception of the news about her father, but he still felt uneasy about her. The way she was reacting wasn't natural, not natural at all. She was only twenty-three, no brothers or sisters, mother dead, and now her father...

There had simply been no one to call on for sympathetic assistance. Her only living relatives were in Scotland, on the opposite side of the world to Sydney, Australia. She didn't even share this terrace house in Paddington with a friend or fellow-nurse while her father was away. It had to be lonely for her. Miserable, in his opinion.

His heart had sunk when she had opened the door to him. She looked so young and vulnerable with those huge blue eyes. Terribly disconcerting... having those eyes fixed on him. He had felt as though he was drowning in them as he'd told her the hard facts of her father's disappearance.

She hadn't cried. Not one tear. He ought to be grateful that she hadn't made the job more distressing, but... it wasn't natural.

'Should we receive any more... er... conclusive news...' he began uncomfortably.

'You'll let me know,' Bethany concluded drily. 'I understand perfectly, Sergeant.'

She saw him out, well aware that he found her attitude puzzling, but too impatient for him to be gone to bother explaining about her father.

Her mind was darting over what had to be done: telephone Singapore Airlines and book the first available flight to Rhafhar; arrange leave of absence from the hospital; get traveller's cheques from the bank; pack clothes; get rid of all perishable foods from the house before locking up...

Bethany wasted no time. She was used to making her own decisions, quickly and firmly, then acting upon them with a single-minded dedication that could not be shaken. At eight years of age she had been told by her gymnast trainer that if she really wanted to compete at international level there was no room for half-heartedness. To succeed she had to be obsessional, and Bethany had applied that teaching to everything she had undertaken.

She had competed at international level, although she had not been good enough to win any medals. Bethany loved gymnastics and still kept up all the exercises, but at sixteen she had faced the fact that age was against her acquiring the extra brilliance that would take her past the twenty-eighth place she had achieved in the world championships. She had gone as far as she could, and it was time to move on to other things.

The interest in her own good health and physical fitness had led her into nursing. Her determination, and a natural inclination to do her best, had made her a highly valued asset to the nursing staff of St Vincent's Hospital, and, when Bethany presented her request to Matron Vaughan that afternoon, it was not well received.

'You want a month's leave? Starting tomorrow?' The eyebrows knitted together, the mouth thinned in vexation, and the battleship bosom heaved in disapproval.

The trainee nurses were all terrified of Matron Vaughan, who demanded nothing less than perfection all the time. She was not only a Tartar on efficiency, but her formidable height and girth gave her a stature that seemed undefiable. Nevertheless, in all her dealings with the matron, Bethany had found her absolutely fair, and had seen many an example of the compassionate heart that beat beneath the iron-clad surface of that impregnable authority.

'Is it a man?' Matron demanded with a flash of alarm.

Bethany smiled. Despite the persistent flirtation from two of the hospital interns, she was heart-whole and fancy-free. In fact, she had never been deeply involved with anyone in an emotional sense, and had sometimes wondered if the disciplined life she had chosen had not made her too self-sufficient. 'No, it's not a man, Matron. Unless you count my father as a man. He needs me.'

Matron relaxed. Sister McGregor was her best theatre nurse. Dr Hong always asked for her when he was doing open-heart surgery. She was steady, dependable, unflappable, and it would be a very real loss to the hospital if she ever left to get married. 'Is your father ill?' she asked with genuine concern.

'He might be,' Bethany sighed, and, as calmly and succinctly as she could, she outlined the situation, aware that Matron had the authority to short-cut the process of getting the medical supplies she needed to take with her.

'But, my dear, you can't go flying off alone to a country like that!' Matron protested.

'I have a list of people to contact when I get there, Matron, and I'm not inexperienced in travelling overseas. Don't worry. I'll cope,' Bethany assured her.

'But the customs . . . the language . . .'

'I can speak some Arabic. My father practised on me before he left. And I know to wear cover-up clothes. I'm not totally unprepared for what I'll meet, believe me.'

Matron shook her head in bemusement. She could read character too well to think she could change Bethany McGregor's mind. The girl might look soft and fragile, but there was steel behind that slight, supple frame. As for coping in a crisis, there was no better nurse on the staff.

A stirring of pride swelled Matron's bosom to flagship proportions. 'I have *always* believed there is *nothing* a woman can't do if she *wants* to, Sister McGregor.'

Bethany grinned at her, relieved that their mutual respect had not been frayed. She could not imagine anyone else of her acquaintance accepting her decision with such aplomb. Indeed, she didn't intend telling anyone else the absolute truth. Listening to a lot of well-meant protests would only waste time.

Matron fixed her with a more purposeful eye. 'And if you get the chance while you're over there, take a tour of one of their hospitals and find out what the working conditions are. I'd be very interested in how they run things. The Arab governments offer an extraordinary amount of money for good medical staff, and I've often wondered...'

She paused, seeing Bethany's look of surprise. 'At my age, my dear, one starts thinking a nest-egg might be handy. But I wouldn't go anywhere that didn't meet my standards.'

Which meant the highest in the world, Bethany thought with private amusement. However, she promised that she would look into the hospital situation if she got the opportunity, and Matron gave Bethany every co-operation in putting together a medical kit which would see her through most emergencies.

Barely twenty-four hours later, Bethany was on a flight to Singapore, the first leg of her journey. She slipped her sneakers off her feet, tilted her economy-class seat back as far as it would go, then, with the ease of long practice, relaxed every muscle in her body. Rest was important after so much concentrated activity, and she did not want to arrive in Rhafhar feeling like a washed-out rag.

The blue and grey striped slacks she wore with a matching long-sleeved shirt were comfortable, and the polyester mix in the fabric meant they would travel well. She had not pinned up her hair, and it frothed around her face and shoulders in an unruly mass of golden-apricot waves. She probably should have had it cut for convenience, but it had taken years to grow to its present length, and it was her one vanity.

The short, Shirley Temple curls of her gymnast years had always been a private vexation to her. Bethany had thought that the weight of long hair would pull out the curls, and it had, for the most part. The cascade effect that her hairdresser had achieved with his scissors was very satisfactory. And the cleverly cut fringe hid her high forehead too, which was just as well since her eyes looked ridiculously large if she scraped her hair back.

She never could work out if the thick sweep of her eyelashes helped the big-eye problem or made it worse, but she was quite sure that her insignificant nose and perky little chin should have had more character. Or something. Her mouth, however, was some consolation: sweetly curved and armed with even white teeth. Bethany had no quarrel at all with her mouth.

And when she flashed a smile at the steward who asked if she would like a drink, he had no quarrel with it, either. In fact, he listed the drinks on offer twice while he drank in all of Bethany's features, finding no fault and much fascination in an arrangement which he considered exquisitely feminine. Despite the number of passengers it was his duty to serve, he found time to return again and again to ask Bethany if he could do anything for her.

It was the first time Bethany had flown across Australia in daylight hours, and by some stroke of good fortune she had been allotted a window-seat. She found the landscape intriguing. Of course, she had seen films of the Outback, but it was only from this height that anyone could appreciate why the centre was called the red heart. It really was red. No greens or greys or earthy neutrals. Just unrelenting red for hundreds and hundreds of miles…a far different type of desert from the one where her father was lost.

For a few moments her heart quailed at the task she had set herself. But who else cared about what happened to her father? He was precious only to her. She would find him. She had to. He was the only person she loved…who loved her.

For the first time since the police sergeant had apprised her of the situation, tears pricked Bethany's eyes. When her mother had died just three months before Bethany was due to compete in the world championships, Douglas McGregor had insisted that his daughter keep training as hard as ever. She would be letting her mother down if she didn't. And somehow the disciplined activity had eased Bethany over her grief.

Two years later, when she was eighteen and accepted as a trainee at St Vincent's Hospital, she had understood her father's decision to take leave from the university and go to New Guinea. Nothing could really fill the hole that his wife's death had left in his life, but it helped to have a mentally stimulating as well as physically demanding project.

Bethany could never forget the hollow loneliness which had eaten through her heart when she had been told he was missing in New Guinea, presumed dead; nor the joyous relief when he had returned to her. She would not let herself despair of ever seeing him again this time. Separation she could bear, but not a final separation. He was not dead. She would not believe it!

'We will be landing at Singapore in approximately fifteen minutes. Landing time is twenty-two thirty. There will be a two-hour stopover at the terminal for those passengers continuing to Dubai on flight SQ38...'

The two-hour wait had to be endured, and Bethany took the opportunity to walk around and stretch her legs. She was astonished and impressed by the sparkling cleanliness of the Singapore airport terminal. Definitely up to Matron Vaughan's standards, she thought approvingly.

She spent most of the stopover browsing through the duty-free shops and, in a moment of pure inspiration, bought a bottle of Johnny Walker *Swing*. Whisky could be a valuable commodity in a country that didn't sell alcohol. Perhaps it would smooth the way when she introduced herself to P.J. Weatherly and asked for his help. The leader of the American archaeological team, which was excavating near al-'Ayn, was certainly the key-man for information concerning her father's last known whereabouts.

Bethany slept for much of the flight to Dubai. It was only one-forty in the morning when the plane landed, although they had been in the air for some six hours. The airbus to Rhafhar was not due to leave until almost six o'clock, but a lot of time was taken up in acquiring a visa for the United Arab

Emirates. Bethany was not part of a tour group, which would have simplified matters, but she finally convinced the authorities she had come to join her father, and P.J. Weatherly's name helped the cause also.

The flight to Rhafhar was mercifully brief—a mere thirty-five-minute hop—and again Bethany was lucky enough to get a window-seat on the airbus. Out to sea she could see the flares of the natural gas fires from the off-shore oil rigs.

Her father had told her that the Trucial States had enjoyed two great periods of prosperity. The first had ended a hundred and fifty years ago, when Great Britain had sent its gunboats in to stop the pirate trade. The second had begun only twenty years before, when huge reserves of oil had been discovered, which turned the seven Emirates of the coast from some of the poorest countries in the world into those among the richest.

An ironic smile twitched at Bethany's mouth. She didn't expect to see much in the way of riches on this trip. But she would have wealth enough if she found her father.

It was a relief when the airbus touched down safely on the tarmac. After sitting passively for so long, Bethany felt the need to get moving. However, the economy-class passengers were held back from disembarking while a curious type of procession left the plane from the first-class compartment.

A number of Arabs surrounded a stretcher-like apparatus which was being carried with almost reverent care. It supported a box-like shape, about a metre square, which was covered by a draping of

black velvet embroidered with gold and silver
thread. Bethany wondered if it was some precious
religious artefact, perhaps a kind of tabernacle.

An excited babble of Arabic broke out among
her fellow passengers, but Bethany's mind was too
occupied with her own plans to concentrate on de-
ciphering what was being said. Once they were allowed to move, she hurried forward so as not to be
held up too long at the official entry barriers.

Fortunately she was quickly passed through, but
then she was caught in an excitable crowd of Arabs
in the reception hall. Bethany tried to barge her
way through, using her heavy handbag to some
effect. However, a sudden surge of movement
trapped her on the edge of a hastily formed avenue
of people, and she was jammed so tightly by the
crush behind and on either side of her that it was
impossible to move, unless she stepped into the
space which had been cleared. And in that space,
right in front of her, sat the stretcher with the velvet-
covered box.

Its guards had obviously ordered the people back,
and now there was a hush of expectancy over the
crowd, necks craning towards the exit of the reception hall. Clearly something or someone important was about to arrive, and Bethany did not
want to put a foot wrong at this critical moment.
She resigned herself to waiting. Despite her impatience to be on her way, she felt a lively curiosity
in whatever ceremony was about to be performed.

She was aware of a wave of deference rippling
through the crowd as a man entered the passageway made for him. He was tall—extremely so for

his race—a head higher than those around him. He wore a white *abba* which covered him from head to foot, and around his shoulders was thrown a black cloak.

The starkness of his attire seemed to accentuate the sheer authority of the man. His face was not really dark, yet there was a fine savagery in its features. He was lean, the spare flesh throwing the high cheekbones and strong jawline into sharp definition. The hooked prominence of his nose declared his heritage, and the thin-lipped mouth held the suggestion of cruel austerity. His eyes were jet-black, deeply set, and disturbingly intense.

An involuntary shiver ran down Bethany's spine. His was the face of a fanatic, or a martyr, or a saint. She could not decide which, but she knew instinctively that the intelligence behind those eyes had the power to sway men's souls. A born leader, who needed no elaborate trappings to imprint his presence on others.

Bethany could not help staring at him as he strode towards both her and the velvet-covered box, and for one disconcerting moment his intense gaze flicked over her. The straight black eyebrows drew briefly together, but in the next instant it seemed she had been summarily dismissed from his mind.

Bethany was conscious of a funny feeling in her heart, as if it had been wrung and released. She found herself holding her breath and expelled it with shaky relief. To this man she could only be another spectator, however oddly she stood out in this crowd of Arabs.

He had come to a halt, his attention fixed entirely on the velvet-covered box, a gleam of avid anticipation in his eyes. He snapped his fingers. A man stepped forward and drew back the cover.

A sigh of awe swept through the crowd. Bethany's hand instinctively rose to her throat to stifle a cry of shock.

The box was not a box, but a cage; and inside the cage was a huge bird, larger than any Bethany had ever seen in her life. It was nearly two feet long and would have to weigh thirty or forty pounds. It was stark white, except for a splash of black trimming on its wingtips. The hooked beak and the heavy talons proclaimed it a bird of prey.

Bethany tore her gaze from the bird to glance sharply at the man, sensing a strong affinity between the two, a primal likeness that went too deep to define, yet it was there. A quiver of shock raced through her body. His attention was no longer fixed on the bird. He was staring with obsessional intent straight at her!

He caught her glance and held it with a force that shook Bethany even more deeply. She could not wrench her gaze away from his, and for the first time in her life she was frightened—really frightened—by a power she didn't understand.

The barest hint of a smile curved his mouth. He raised his hand in a signal, and the velvet cloth was replaced over the cage. He snapped his fingers. The carriers picked up their burden and went on their way. The crowd dispersed immediately, seeming to shrink away from Bethany as the man stepped towards her.

'Did the falcon frighten you?'

His voice was soft, almost musical, not at all what Bethany had expected from such a man. A harsh, guttural tone would have seemed more in keeping. Yet it still commanded an answer from her, and Bethany strove her utmost to pull her wits together.

'He is an awesome creature; but no, it would take more than that to frighten me,' she replied, an unconscious note of proud defiance creeping into her voice. She had never before been intimidated by a man, and she didn't intend to be affected by the force of this man's charismatic power now.

Again came that faint twitch of his lips that might or might not have been a smile. 'It is not a he. Males are tiercels. Properly speaking, only females can be falcons. They are bigger, heavier, swifter, more deadly on the hunt. And the one you saw was a great Greenland gyrfalcon, the queen of them all. Such a bird is beyond price.'

Despite her resolution to show no weakness, Bethany shivered. 'You make it sound so brutal.'

'All of life is brutal,' he observed mockingly, but the intensity of his gaze was unnerving as he added, 'Who are you? What are you doing here?'

Bethany didn't even think of refusing to answer. 'My name is Bethany Lyon McGregor. And I've come to find my father, Douglas MacArthur McGregor.'

He paused for a moment, his brow knotting into lines of concentrated thought. When he spoke again, his voice was almost a whisper. 'So, you are the daughter of the dead man.'

Alarm, and, for the first time ever, panic, crashed through Bethany, followed by a gigantic wave of despair, crushing and drowning everything that gave her life purpose. The floor and the room performed a dizzying spiral, and for one sickening moment Bethany thought she was going to commit the ultimate disgrace and faint.

The hands of the Arab reached out and touched her lightly on the top of her shoulders, not enough to even steady her, yet a pulse of electrical charge spiked through her body. Her legs felt as if they would buckle beneath her, her skin felt clammy and her breath came in short, painful gasps.

'How do you know this?' The words had to be forced out over a tongue that felt as unwieldy as a thick sponge. 'Who are you?'

'I am the ruler of Bayrar, and it is my duty as sheikh to know everything that happens in my kingdom. And outside it, as well. I was informed that P.J. Weatherly sent a telex to your government on the matter. I wondered what would happen.' He looked at her intently. 'Now I know.'

He took a half-pace towards her, closing the gap between them. His fingers, as light as silk, felt the muscles at the back of her neck, tracing the line of tension to her skull. For one wild, erratic moment, Bethany thought he was discovering things about her with his fingertips that speech would never reveal.

'You have found my father's body?'

Her speech was slurred as if she was drunk, but Bethany never took alcoholic drinks. It affected the timing and rhythm of her gymnastics. She forced the words out because she had to be completely sure. If she could actually see her father's body...she had to see him...one last time...

'No. There is no need. The dead disappear all too easily in the area where your father was working. To find a body would be most unusual.'

An enormous weight suddenly lifted from Bethany's chest. Her breathing returned quickly to normal, her pulse steadied to its usual, even pace. There was no body! It was all supposition!

She took a step backwards from the Arab, needing to separate herself from the disturbing power of his touch. The hands slid from her shoulders and dropped to his side. She had the oddest sensation that she had just lost the most vibrant contact she had ever experienced throughout her life. The feeling of aloneness jarred Bethany.

But she *was* alone, she reasoned frantically. This Arab was not going to help her to find a man he believed dead. It was up to her, and she wasn't going to permit anything or anyone to get in her way.

'As far as I'm concerned, my father is not dead until I see his body. Nothing else will ever convince me.' Her chin jutted forward defiantly as she waited for his response.

'Your conviction cannot alter the truth,' he said confidently.

'No!' Bethany reiterated. 'Missing does not mean dead!'

'It does when the lifeline of communication is discontinued. This country is not like your own world, Bethany Lyon McGregor.'

He raised his hand when she would have protested again, and Bethany automatically obeyed the
gesture for silence.

'It is not known what actually happened to your
father, but there are a number of possibilities which
are all too real. Life is not considered so precious
here.'

He started ticking off the points on his fingers;
long, supple fingers that would play musical instruments with great skill, or touch people with a
sensitive probing that told him more than words
ever would. Bethany found herself mesmerised by
them as he spoke on.

'The roving tribes of Bedouin might take the
notion of killing a lone foreigner as a good idea.
There is the Shihuh—the blue-eyed people your
father was studying—he may have offended them.
The bands of robbers; the caravan people; the
Marxist guerrillas from Yemen. Any, or all of them,
may have been involved. Do you want me to go
on?'

Each prospect he outlined was enough to send a
chill through Bethany's heart; and the sum of them
was a daunting case against her father's survival.
But she clung to her faith in her father's resource-
fulness. Douglas MacArthur McGregor would
never be an easy victim to anything. Bethany knew
he was far more than a scholar. He was tough and
determined and endlessly clever.

She shook her head, more to rid herself of the
sheikh's uncanny influence than in answer to his
question.

'I'll find him,' she declared in stubborn rejection of everything he had said. 'I'll go up into the Jebel Hafit mountains . . .'

'You . . . will . . . not!' Each word was spoken with a slow, deliberate emphasis to reinforce his meaning. His tone was autocratic, and Bethany was breathlessly aware that this man was not used to being disobeyed.

It did not change her resolve. She glared her defiance. 'Yes, I will! I haven't travelled a third of the way around the world just to . . .'

'You will do exactly as you are told,' he interrupted, every word as cold as if it had been frozen in ice. He was leaving no possibility of any future misunderstanding between them. 'Until the generation of my father,' he continued, 'only two white men had ever been in that part of the world throughout all of history. It is rough, uncivilised, dangerous . . .'

'Of course it is,' Bethany interjected impatiently. He was really being difficult. 'That is why it is so important to an anthropologist. That's why Dad went there. Where else in the world are there tribes and races that have virtually never been heard of?'

Her petulant outburst brought a hard stoniness to his face. The intense black eyes glittered at her without compassion or charity. The soft voice took on a whip-like edge.

'In consideration of your journey, I will allow you to go to the oasis of al-'Ayn where you may talk to P.J. Weatherly. He may have further information about your father's life before he died that

will be of interest to you. After that, you will return
to Rhafhar. Nothing else is permitted.'

'You can't do that,' Bethany blustered. 'You have
no right . . .'

'I have every right,' the Arab said without
emotion. 'I am the law. I am the justice. I am absolute monarch. And my authority is absolute. It
is the will of Allah. Do as you are told, Bethany
Lyon McGregor. I will not be disobeyed.'

There was no way Bethany was going to do what
he had told her, but it would be completely
undiplomatic for her to say so right at this moment.
'Yes,' she said meekly. 'I will go to al-'Ayn.'

His lips once more twitched in that smile that
was not quite a smile. 'We will make sure...of your
safety,' he murmured, and, without waiting for any
further comment from Bethany, he swung on his
heel and strode off.

An escort of men quickly fell in behind him.
Bethany had not even noticed them standing nearby
while the sheikh had been speaking to her. Her
whole attention had been drawn by him, focused
on him to the exclusion of all else. A powerful man,
impossible to ignore . . . but he was gone now.

The lingering sense of his presence disturbed her
for several moments before she determinedly
shrugged it off. The stiffening of her spine and the
squaring of her shoulders were merely physical
manifestations of the mental effort required to
dismiss his words and orders. Mutiny stirred again,
and she deliberately fed it with resentments.

She was not going to be ordered off.

She was not going to be pushed around, ignored, dismissed, or patronised.

She was going to find her father!

CHAPTER TWO

RE-ARMED with steely purpose, Bethany marched over to collect her suitcase from the luggage carousel which was already in motion. She did not have long to wait. As she was reaching out to pick up her bag from the moving belt, another—and darker—hand lifted it off ahead of her.

'That's mine!' she cried indignantly, swinging around to find a strange Arab standing beside her.

He was short and thin, and the grey in his eyebrows added age to the weathered lines of his face. He gave her a bow of acknowledgement, but did not relinquish the suitcase. 'I am here to help you,' he said in a low, gravelly voice.

An opportunist porter intent on an easy tip, Bethany concluded; but he might be useful. Undoubtedly his brother or son or cousin would have a hire-car waiting for the passenger he would steer their way. Her father had described such a system in his letters.

'Thank you. I do need some help,' she frankly admitted.

A suspiciously indulgent smile hovered on the man's lips as he spoke with precise politeness. 'Prince Zakr Tahnun Sadiq sends his compliments. He has assigned me to drive you to al-'Ayn, Miss McGregor. And also to bring you back again. If you will follow me...'

Bethany's heart abruptly sank as she remembered the last words spoken to her by the sheikh who had come for the falcon. 'We will make sure...of your safety.' She certainly hadn't expected this direct interference with her plans. And why the devil should he interfere? He hadn't cared about her father and he couldn't care about her, either.

'Just who is Prince Zakr?' she demanded in exasperation.

'He is the Sheikh of Bayrar. And I am his servant,' the Arab answered with distinct respect. No matter if the sheikh was of minor or major importance in the administration of this country, it was clear that this man was not about to disobey his prince.

Bethany hesitated. For the present she was caught in a trap. The Arab had her suitcase firmly in his grasp. She either had to fight him for it or fall in with the arrangement made by the sheikh; an arrangement he had undoubtedly made with another snap of his fingers. Well, at least he didn't mean her any harm, Bethany decided, and she wouldn't get anywhere at all if she started arguing.

'How kind he is!' she said with the sweetest smile she could compose. 'Please lead on. I am very grateful for your assistance.'

Spy or guard or driver, whatever this man was, the best way to disarm his vigilance on her was to appear compliant to the sheikh's will. Bethany followed him with an air of happy relief that the problem of transport had been pleasantly resolved.

The old man led her to an enormous black limousine, and Bethany couldn't help grinning to herself as the door was opened for her and she sank into a plush, contoured leather seat. Against all her expectations she was experiencing oil-wealth, after all.

But only while it suited her, she vowed in silent but very fixed determination. She wanted to get to al-'Ayn anyway, but as for being brought back again... Bethany had other plans. Sooner or later she would have to shake off this driver who had been put in charge of her; but the first step was to get to P.J. Weatherly. A lot depended on what that gentleman could tell her. He was the first link in her quest to find her father.

A four-lane highway streaked through the desert for some ninety miles from Rhafhar, giving Bethany an assurance that she was not so far from modern civilisation as the Sheikh of Bayrar would have her believe. Nevertheless, she could not entirely discount what he had told her, nor dispel the dread that he might be right about her father.

But she couldn't give up. Wouldn't. No matter how weighty the circumstantial evidence was, it was still circumstantial, not positive proof. She knew her father would feel exactly the same if it were she who was missing.

For as long as Bethany remembered, she and her father had shared a very special empathy. Often only a glance or a smile was enough to tell her what he was thinking, without a word being spoken. Since her mother's death seven years ago, when Bethany had taken over the running of their home in Paddington, that closeness had been reinforced with her father sharing his work with her: his dreams, his enthusiasm, his passion for learning about people and lost cultures.

He wasn't dead, Bethany recited to herself with earnest conviction. She didn't care what anyone else said. No one knew her father as well as she did, certainly not the Sheikh of Bayrar. And she was not going to let him or anyone else put her off her purpose.

It took nearly two hours to reach their destination, and the limousine slowed as they approached al-'Ayn. It was only one of seven towns scattered throughout the oasis, and Bethany was further impressed by the modern construction of the buildings: all reinforced concrete. The traditional mud-brick housing was non-existent.

'Do they make concrete here?' she asked in surprised comment.

'No. It's brought from Rhafhar,' the driver told her.

'That must be expensive,' Bethany mused.

'Not as expensive as what was used before,' came the grim observation. 'Mud is too precious to be wasted on building houses. It is needed for growing fruit and vegetables.'

It was a sober reminder that money didn't necessarily buy survival in a desert country.

'Do you wish to go to the European compound to sleep after your long trip?' she was asked. 'Or would you rather go out to the grave tumuli that the Americans are excavating?'

The question was a clear indication that the sheikh had circumscribed her movements to one or the other of these specified areas. Bethany fought down a wave of belligerence. It would not serve her purpose to show the driver that she didn't accept the sheikh's word as law, particularly when that word encompassed her father's supposed death.

'Please take me to the dig,' she instructed firmly. As tired as she felt, she couldn't afford to waste time sleeping.

The driver accelerated up the broad street of the town and out into the desert. After a few miles they turned up a narrow track that led on to a plateau.

Bethany's gaze swept around in incredulous amazement. Graves, the driver had said, and there were thousands upon thousands of them: neat, circular mounds of stone, like small, gravel hillocks. Most of them looked to be between six to ten feet in height, and crowded so closely together that their footings overlapped in some places. It was the weirdest landscape Bethany had ever seen.

'Incredible!' she murmured.

It drew an amused grin from her driver. 'Many people were buried here during the Age of Ignorance.'

He steered a careful route over a rutted track between the walls of rock and stone until they came to a tumulus where several men were working on an excavation. The car came to an abrupt halt. Bethany thanked the driver and got out.

The black limousine had drawn a few curious glances, but Bethany's appearance triggered an instant flurry of activity. Men seemed to spring from everywhere, all eager to help her. Bethany surmised that white women were an uncommon occurrence in this part of the desert.

'I'd like to speak to Mr P.J. Weatherly,' she en-
quired of one sun-bronzed young man in his early
twenties.

'Sure.' The American accent was unmistakable.
'I'll be happy to take you to him. Only a short
walk.'

The wave of his hand directed Bethany's attention to a tent which had been previously obscured from her view by the mounds beside the
track. Several jeeps were parked next to it. Even as
she accepted the friendly escort offer, a white-haired
man emerged from the tent and stared down the
road at her.

'Ah! There he is now!' The young man threw her
a grin. 'We don't get too many visitors in limou-
sines. I guess someone popped into the tent and
alerted P.J.'

And P.J. Weatherly did not look pleased at the
sight of her, Bethany thought. His beetling frown
expressed irritation at this uninvited disruption to
work. As he strode towards them, Bethany was fast
figuring out how to get him on her side. He was a
big man with a slight paunch, and his white hair
extended down his florid cheeks to form a pointed
beard. She hoped he liked whisky.

'P.J. Weatherly, ma'am,' he said in curt self-
introduction, hard blue eyes dismissing the man at
her side as he offered his hand to Bethany. 'What
can I do for you?'

'Bethany McGregor, Mr Weatherly,' she coun-
tered just as succinctly. 'I understand you were in
contact with my father, Douglas McGregor, before
he went missing.'

Shock and dismay flitted across his face, quickly followed by a settling of deep concern. He patted her hand in awkward sympathy. 'My dear girl...you've come all this way...from Australia?'

'I want to find my father,' Bethany stated categorically. 'I'd appreciate your telling me everything you can about his last-known situation.'

He chewed his lower lip, then cast a frowning look at his team of workers, who were still feasting their eyes on Bethany's femininity. 'We can't talk here. Better if I meet you tonight. Where are you staying?'

Bethany's huge eyes filled with luminous appeal. 'Actually, I'd appreciate your advice on that, Mr Weatherly...'

'P.J. Everyone calls me P.J.'

Her smile was infinitely disturbing when he had nothing good to tell her.

'Please call me Bethany,' she said. 'And the fact is, I have nowhere to stay yet. I only flew in to Rhafhar this morning, and I've driven straight here. Prince Zakr...' she couldn't recall the rest of his name '...the Sheikh of Bayrar lent me his car.'

'Good God!'

The realisation—however false it was—that she had friends in high places, had the effect that Bethany wanted. P.J. Weatherly instantly offered her the use of his apartment in the European compound, gave her the key, told her to help herself to any food and drink she liked, and advised her to have a good restful sleep for the remainder of the day.

He saw her back into the limousine, gave instructions to her driver, and could not have been more avuncular as he assured her that they would have a long talk when he got home after the day's dig had been completed.

Bethany was not averse to this plan. She needed to get herself established in what the sheikh's man would consider a safe place. He drove her to P.J.'s apartment block and carried in her suitcase. Bethany bestowed another sweet smile on him.

'Thank you so much. I'll be staying here for a few days. I'm sure Mr Weatherly will look after any transport I might need,' she said with every air of careless confidence, fiercely hoping that it would shake the man off her back.

'I am to wait on your convenience, Miss McGregor,' came the polite but unmistakably relentless answer.

Bethany hid her frustration, thanked him again and firmly closed him out of the apartment, wishing she could close him out of her mind. He was a complication that had to be bypassed one way or another if she was ever to get into the mountain region where her father had been working.

However, she had achieved her first aim—P.J. Weatherly was being most co-operative—and that was cause for some satisfaction.

It was a two-bedroom apartment, comfortably furnished but as cluttered as her father's rooms at home: papers and books everywhere, but clean underneath it all. In the kitchen was a large basket of tempting fruit: mangoes, figs, grapes and bananas. And the cupboards contained lots of tinned food and packets of biscuits.

Bethany made herself a cup of coffee and nibbled a few biscuits as she drank it. She wasn't really hungry. It was difficult to control the sense of urgency that had been increased tenfold since the sheikh had spelled out the possibilities of what might have happened to her father.

If he had been taken prisoner... if he was being maltreated... surviving in a hostile environment was one thing, but she was all too aware of how cruel people could be.

But worrying about unknowns was not going to help her in her quest. Since there was nothing more that could be done until P.J. Weatherly came home, she unpacked a fresh change of clothes, had a long, leisurely shower, then stretched out on what she judged to be the spare bed and did the relaxation exercises that would put her to sleep. At least when she obtained all the information she could from P.J., she would be ready for action.

It was late evening when she awoke, almost dark. Bethany quickly rose, dressed in the khaki slacks and white shirt she had laid out, pushed a brush through her hair, and ventured out to the living-room, where she found her host poring over some drawings which were spread over the table.

'Ah!' he said as he glanced up and spotted her. 'Feeling better now?'

'Yes, thank you,' Bethany smiled at him.

He immediately looked uncomfortable, and got up to bustle around the kitchen, fussing about her dinner. He had already eaten himself, but he had a cold meal all prepared for her. On the other hand, if she would like a drink first...

Bethany produced the bottle of whisky, and his eyes lit up with pleasure. 'Strictly forbidden, you know,' he remarked, but he eagerly reached for glasses, and didn't protest at all when Bethany demurred in favour of the Coca Cola that was stocked in his refrigerator.

Bethany ate the dinner he set in front of her, answering P.J.'s questions about herself until all such civilities had been exhausted and he was more at ease with her. By that time the bottle of Johnny Walker *Swing* had induced a more affable mood in the archaeologist. Concealing her own painful urgency to know all he could tell her, Bethany tactfully led him into the subject of her father's disappearance.

'It wasn't the supplies so much as his letter to you that made me think something had to be wrong. He talked about you a lot, Bethany. Very proud of you. Never missed giving me a letter to post to you every month. Wouldn't have mattered if he went much longer without renewing supplies, but he wouldn't have missed sending you his news...' P.J. sadly shook his head. 'Had to be something wrong.'

He took a deep swig of whisky. 'Told the officials in town. They're good about checking on foreigners. They went out to his location in the Jebel Hafit mountains, but there was no sign of him. Gone as if he'd never existed. The Shihuh tribe that had inhabited the caves were all gone, too. Nobody there. All cleaned out. Just as though they had all been wiped off the face of the earth,' he added in a maudlin murmur.

'He would have survived,' Bethany said with quiet force. 'We were so close...'

P.J. winced as he lifted his gaze to meet hers, hating to kill the light of faith in those large, beautiful eyes. 'I'm afraid the case is hopeless, my dear.'

Fear and despair clutched once more at her heart, but Bethany held grimly to her resolution. She refused to believe that there was no hope.

'I wish it were not so,' P.J. sighed. 'But...' He went on to reiterate the same possibilities that the sheikh had outlined.

It only served to steel Bethany's purpose. She was not prepared to accept such intangible evidence for her father's death. She had been a nurse too long not to know there were startling exceptions to every rule.

She listened politely, hiding her inner agitation as she coped with the realisation that the archaeologist was not going to help her. Like the sheikh, he believed that her father was dead. So she was on her own. And, if that was the case, she needed all her wits to use any ploy or persuasion that could get her where she wanted to go.

She did not repeat her earlier mistake with the sheikh of showing her disbelief, or revealing her determination to pursue the matter further. When P.J.'s exposition finally dwindled into a grave silence, Bethany asked if he could show her on a map where exactly her father had been in the Jebel Hafit mountains.

P.J. seemed relieved by the request, bustling around to find the most detailed map of the region, then pointing out the approximate location of her father's cave-base.

'I would like to go there tomorrow,' Bethany said quietly, hoping that P.J. would see her need and co-operate.

He coughed. 'It's a long way. A hundred and twenty miles. Mostly over desert. In the mountains there are only goat tracks. Four hours there...four hours back. Not much point to it, Bethany.'

'I still want to go, P.J.,' Bethany pressed. 'I have to see where Daddy...' The thought of what her father might be suffering was enough to bring a sheen of tears to her eyes.

P.J. cleared his own throat. 'My dear, of course I understand. Perfectly natural. I wish I could take you, but ... time is so pressing. If I'm not here, the dig cannot continue... No good would be served by going...'

'I wouldn't expect *you* to come, P.J.,' Bethany put in hurriedly. 'I thought perhaps...could I borrow your jeep for the day?' Her eyes lifted imploringly.

As he took stock of what she was asking, a ponderous frown descended on his brow, worse than the one she had seen this morning. He poured himself another drink, and wearily shook his head.

'To go off alone! By yourself! No, my dear girl, that's madness! Only God knows what happened to your father, and I can't permit you to take such a risk. Wouldn't do at all. Dangerous country.'

He chewed his lower lip for several moments before his expression lightened. 'The sheikh's man downstairs—you'll have to come to some arrangement with him. He's here to look after you. Told me so when I questioned him this evening.'

Bethany could hardly hide her disappointment. All her hopes had lain with getting P.J.'s help in going to the site, and evading the Arab. There was no way the driver would help her. The Sheikh of Bayrar had put him on to her as a watch dog.

However, she couldn't afford to waste time wallowing in disappointment. P.J. had made up his mind and left her with no leeway to work on changing it. Which meant she had to act without his assistance. She needed another plan, and fast!

P.J.'s eyes narrowed in curious speculation. 'You've got a very powerful friend in Prince Zakr Tahnun Sadiq, Bethany.'

'Yes,' she replied, grateful that the kindly old archaeologist completely misread the situation between herself and the prince. If he knew the truth of the situation he would be bundling her up and sending her back to Rhafhar. And that would be the end of Douglas McGregor.

On the other hand, he had already downed a fair portion of the whisky in the bottle. If she could get him drunk, she might be able to steal his jeep for the day. This plan was about as desperate as they came, but nothing else would suffice now. She refilled his glass, then steered the conversation away from her own sensitive position by getting P.J. to talk on his favourite subject—the grave-mounds that he was excavating.

Some considerable time later, and with subtle encouragement from Bethany, the whisky bottle was empty and P.J. declared his intention of rolling into bed. 'Should sleep through the prayer-call tonight,' he remarked with satisfaction.

'What prayer-call?' Bethany queried.

'The *muezzin*—or local priest—calls all the faithful to prayer just before the crack of dawn. It's a God-almighty sound. Uses a loud speaker in the top of the minaret of the mosque. Feel like shooting him sometimes.' He patted her hand indulgently. 'Don't worry about it, my dear. Try to have a good rest. Your father...very proud of you. Very proud. Rightly so...'

Bethany did not go to bed. She'd had enough sleep to see her through another twenty-four hours, and there was a lot of problems to think about. She did not doubt that her father was gone from the Jebel Hafit mountains. If he was not dead—and Bethany stubbornly shut her mind to the possibility that he was—he had most probably been taken away by force.

Douglas McGregor was very smart, very intelligent. If he had any chance at all, and was not taken completely by surprise, he would have left some clue about his abductors; and that was what she had to look for.

Bethany put the final touches to her plan of action and went to work, gathering together everything she would need, and whatever else she thought might come in handy. She hoped P.J. wouldn't mind her petty pilfering. Considering the amount of alcohol he had consumed, he should not wake up until she was long gone. And then it would be too late. When she was ready she turned off the lights, lay down on her bed, and waited.

At three o'clock she rose and made herself some breakfast by torchlight. Having eaten and cleaned up afterwards, she put on the many-pocketed battle-jacket that matched her slacks. These were the clothes she wore on camping trips with her father, and just wearing them made Bethany feel more confident. Hadn't her father shown her every sur-vival skill he had ever learnt on their camping trips? He knew how to look after his life. And he'd fight to keep it.

Just hold on, Dad, she thought fiercely. I'm coming.

She shoved the torch into one of the bottom pockets, and tucked her sunglasses into a breast pocket for easy reach when needed. The medical supplies that she and Matron Vaughan had packed in Sydney were already in the carry-all bag, along with the food and mineral water. Bethany re-checked everything in her mind. There was nothing left to do except wait.

Her watch showed a few minutes past four when the prayer-call began. She hoped it would hide the noise of starting the motor.

She quickly jammed her hat on her head, col-lected her large handbag and the carry-all, picked up the all-important key that she had lifted from P.J.'s bedside table, and silently let herself out of the apartment.

The grey light of dawn revealed that the black limousine was empty. The prayer-call had risen to a loud wail. A furtive look up and down the street assured Bethany that the sheikh's man was no-where in sight. She slung her bags into the back of the jeep that was parked behind the limousine, then checked that the spare fuel and water cans were full. Which they were.

She climbed quickly into the driver's seat. The key slotted smoothly into the ignition. With a hopeful prayer that the engine would respond im-mediately, she turned the key and very gently pressed her foot on the accelerator.

Much to Bethany's relief and elation, everything worked like a dream. The fuel-gauge read full, and she eased the vehicle out of the compound. No one came running after her. Confident now of a clean getaway, she sped off along the route she had mem-orised from P.J.'s maps.

Not a soul attempted to stop and question her. With her khaki slacks and battle-jacket, and her hair tucked up under the cloth army hat, she could pass for a man in the dim light; pass for a man later on, too, if no one looked closely at her.

She hoped P.J. wouldn't miss his vehicle too much for just one day. Surely he could get someone to give him a lift, or even badger the Arab to take him out to the dig in the black limousine? The thought made Bethany smile, but she assured herself P.J. would be quite all right after he got over his hangover. And after all, the cost to him was negligible compared to what might happen to her father if she didn't find him.

Once Bethany had put the town well behind her, she placed the jeep in four-wheel drive, took a compass reading, and headed out over the sand into the desert. She could see the Jebel Hafit mountains as a sort of haze on the horizon. All she had to do was head for them, then drive along the foothills. However, she had to be sure of finding her way back, so Bethany paid careful attention to the compass and odometer reading.

The driving was exhilarating in the cool of the morning, and, for the first time since the police sergeant had come with his news, Bethany felt confident of a line to work on. If the caves yielded any evidence at all that her father might still be alive, she would do her damnedest to force more action out of officialdom.

It took Bethany about an hour to reach the foothills of the Jebel Hafit mountains. Only then did she appreciate how massive they were. They seemed to sweep upwards into the clouds.

Bethany stopped the jeep and built a little cairn of rocks to guide her when she returned this way. She examined the location of the caves on the map once more, took another reading of the compass, and, quite certain that she would have no difficulty retracing her steps, she struck out in the direction that would give her the shortest route to her destination.

From a distance, some of the desert looked like savannah grasslands, but Bethany soon realised that was an illusion. Up close there was only a blade of grass every yard or two. She carefully skirted a flat area which might or might not have been a *sabakha*. Her father had written that those salt flats could

be very firm or impossibly boggy. She was not
taking any unnecessary risks.

The mountains were very close, and Bethany was
nursing a triumphant sense of achievement as she
drove over a dune...and straight into a mounted
band of Arab soldiers. Automatic reaction slammed
her foot on the brakes. Then, as the jeep skidded
to a halt, Bethany realised in appalled horror that
she should have kept on driving, no matter what!
A jeep could outspeed and outlast a horse.

Too late now, she acknowledged with a sinking
heart. The men had surrounded the jeep. And they
had guns! A rapid-fire discussion was held. Bethany
was too shaken by the situation to take it in. One
of the men dismounted and motioned her to move
into the passenger seat.

Bethany did her best to assume an air of independent authority as she sat firm. 'My name is
Bethany Lyon McGregor...'

The Arab picked her up and dumped her into the
passenger seat before Bethany could even utter another word, and she was scorchingly conscious of
the laughter which this action evoked.

'The Sheikh of Bayrar will hear of this!' Bethany
shrilled in Arabic, dredging up the one name she
knew which might put the fear of Allah into these
fierce-looking men.

The usurper of the driving-wheel grinned at her.
'Indeed he will. And very soon,' he said, evoking
more laughter with the words.

He started the engine with a full-throttled roar,
and the jeep took off with the mounted escort in
full gallop on either side of it. There was absolutely

nothing that Bethany could do but sit tight and try to stop her head from filling with all sorts of horrible possibilities.

The last thing she needed now was a jammed-up mind! She had only her wits to save her from...well, she wasn't going to think about what she had to save herself from, until she knew quite definitely what it was. At least they hadn't shot her. And they hadn't hurt her, either. Only her pride. A bit.

She decided to obey their next order without argument and with good grace. Of course, that did rather depend on what the next order was. There were some things... She wished she could stop her heart from beating with such painful intensity.

The jeep topped a ridge, and Bethany could not repress a shiver of apprehension as she saw some sort of camp only a hundred yards or so away. Several trucks and cars were parked next to a large tent. A group of men were seated on a carpet laid out in front of the tent, and this was flanked by a bodyguard of soldiers. To one side there were perches set up, and on these sat huge falcons, similar to the one Bethany had seen at Rhafhar.

The mounted escort peeled away from the jeep as it slowed to a halt. The driver leapt out and made an elaborate courtesy of handing Bethany down to the ground, grinning at her all the while. Bethany was very, very aware that she had become the focus of attention for all the soldiers standing by, and tried to walk with stiff dignity as she was led towards the group seated on the carpet.

Her heart started catapulting around her chest the moment she recognised the central figure. The black eyes fastened on her with a recognition as instant as her own, and Bethany wondered bleakly what the punishment was for disobeying the absolute authority of the Sheikh of Bayrar.

CHAPTER THREE

PRINCE ZAKR TAHNUN SADIQ rose slowly and all too majestically to his feet. He wore a red and blue *taub* which threw the commanding austerity of his face into even sharper relief. His companions stood and moved aside, leaving him in sole, towering authority.

The soldier at Bethany's side spoke, but there was no longer any merriment in his voice or manner. He told his story succinctly... This woman had been found driving across the hunting grounds. When apprehended, she had named the sheikh himself as her protector. A foreign woman travelling alone in the desert had seemed suspicious, so the soldiers had agreed she should be brought to the camp. That was all.

Prince Zakr was definitely not amused. The black eyes bored into hers with a cold ferocity that sent a shiver down Bethany's spine. She wished she had bitten off her tongue before she had committed such a hopeless indiscretion as calling on the sheikh's name to aid her in her predicament. If she had obeyed him, she wouldn't be in any predicament at all, and they both knew it.

'You wished an audience with me, Miss McGregor?' Each crisp, sarcastic word sounded like fine crystal smashing into tiny fragments.

Bethany swallowed hard. 'I...er...apologise, very sincerely, for interrupting your...ah...hunting...' What did she call him? Prince? Sheikh? Zakr? Mister? '...Your Majesty...' That couldn't be too far wrong, Bethany thought wildly. She scrutinised his features to see if the flattering address had elicited any change of expression. There was none.

'I'm sure you regret your mistake,' was the softly cutting reply. 'If not now, then by the time I've finished teaching you.'

Bethany bitterly revised her first impression of Prince Zakr Tahnun Sadiq. He was certainly not a saint nor a martyr. He was a devil, a fanatical devil, to boot!

Apologies were obviously out. With an intense concentration sharpened by sheer desperation, Bethany sifted through all the options she had left, and dredged a wild card idea out of her mind. She wasn't sure it could stand too much scrutiny, but she played it with all the conviction of her own cause.

'I had to find you!' she cried in impassioned appeal. 'I had to see you!'

One eyebrow lifted marginally. 'You came here...looking for me?'

Bethany plunged on, ignoring the silky edge of incredulity in his question. 'You did say that you were the law,' she reminded him. 'And also the dispenser of justice. And that's precisely what I need to find my father. Justice!' she repeated with righteous fervour.

For a moment he stared at her as if he had never seen her before; as if she was a stranger who had just shed a cloak that he had known and measured. Then his mouth curled in a dry little half-smile that was almost whimsical, except there was no whimsy in his eyes. None at all. There was something very disturbing about the look in his eyes. It made Bethany's heart skitter all over the place.

'It is not my custom to receive petitioners so informally, Miss McGregor,' he stated with a quiet tonelessness that gave Bethany no hint of what he was thinking. 'However, since you are a visitor to our country, and the circumstances are . . . extraordinary . . . I shall make an exception in your case, and grant you a private audience.'

He half turned and one of his attendants darted forward to hold open the tent-flap. The sheikh gestured an invitation for Bethany to precede him.

She took a deep breath in an attempt to calm her erratic pulse, then walked quickly through the lines of watching men, relieved to be out of the limelight, but no less apprehensive about facing the sheikh alone. That faintly derisive intonation on 'extraordinary' was still ringing in her ears. She was not out of the woods yet, not by any stretch of the imagination.

'As my guest, you will, of course, have the ritual three cups of coffee,' he said as Bethany brushed past him, and it was more a command than an enquiry.

It stopped her close to him, forcing her to turn and meet his eyes, and suddenly she felt the full blast of the power she was defying. Every instinct

in her body screeched alarms. This man was unlike
any other she had met . . . a sharp, intuitive intelligence burning within steel-like strength.

Bethany's courage quailed for a moment, and she
meekly nodded her assent. Then she wrenched her
gaze from his and stepped forward into the tent,
struggling to reassert her sense of personal freedom.
She didn't belong to him. She didn't have to do
what he said. She had every right to order her own
life.

She heard him clap his hands twice, then the
slight smack of the tent-flap falling shut, and, as
much as she tried to ignore the overwhelming sense
of his presence just behind her, Bethany was hopelessly, helplessly aware of it. Only with a concentrated demand on her will-power did she register
the contents of the tent.

Clearly it was a temporary shade-place for the
hunting party to eat and drink. Several long trestle
tables were set up with a plentiful number of fold-
up chairs. Directly in front of her was a smaller
table, covered by an embroidered cloth, and sur-
rounding this table were comfortable cane chairs,
amply padded with rich cushions.

'You may now take off that most unbecoming
hat, Miss McGregor. It offends me.'

Her nerves were so taut that she almost jumped
when he spoke, and she whipped her hat off so fast
that half her hairpins were dislodged. 'Oh!' she
gasped in vexed embarrassment, one hand scrabbling to catch the tumbling locks.

'Allow me.'

Bethany froze in petrified shock as his hands probed her hair, removing all her pins. His fingers raked through the rippling waves, fanning them out around her face. His touch seemed to electrify every nerve in her body, and she barely stopped herself from gaping up at him as he handed her the hairpins.

His eyes held a faint glitter of mockery. 'If you wanted to pass as a boy, you really should have worn sunglasses.'

'I have them in my jacket pocket. It was barely dawn when I left...' She bit down on the words. His nearness was rattling her into admissions she hadn't intended to make.

His finger lightly brushed her chin. 'Even then, I would have recognised you. There is more to you than meets the eye. Even more than I had anticipated. And I pride myself on being able to read a person's character.'

The glitter in his eyes disappeared into a darkness that seemed to swallow her up. His finger moved upwards, slowly tracing the line of her full lower lip. 'I do not believe that you came looking for me, Bethany Lyon McGregor. Abdul would have been with you.'

'Abdul?' She almost choked over the word, her throat was so dry. Her tongue automatically licked out to reduce the tingling sensation caused by his tantalising touch.

His gaze dropped to her mouth. Bethany sucked in her lower lip, her small, even teeth biting over it to keep it from quivering. This man was drawing physical reactions from her that were completely outside her experience. Rendering her mind incapable of sensible thought. She even caught herself wondering what it would be like to have his lips moving softly over her own, her eyes closed and . . .

'The driver I sent you. What did you do with him?'

The finger moved again, brushing softly over her cheek, then delicately caressing the curl of her ear. Bethany could barely stop herself from gasping. Driver, she thought frantically.

'I didn't do anything with him. He wasn't there,' she blurted out in a rush.

The finger dropped away. His eyes lifted to hers, hard black coals of judgement. 'Abdul will be called to account for his negligence in carrying out my orders.'

'Oh, no!' The protest was wrung from Bethany. 'You can't blame him. I . . .' She saw the slight twitch of his lips and stopped.

'You were surprisingly resourceful,' he said for her.

'Yes,' she whispered, a flush of angry shame washing into her cheeks. He had trapped her, defeated her without a defensive blow being struck, merely by mesmerising her with his touch. What on earth was the matter with her that she should be so hopelessly gullible?

He stared at her for several long, spine-tingling minutes. 'Why don't you simply admit you were heading for the Jebel Hafit mountains, despite my orders to the contrary?'

'I never denied it!' Bethany retorted hotly, and then took a firm grip on herself. 'Nor do I consider it just that you should exercise such a form of tyranny over me. Is it fair that you should block my way to finding my father?'

He frowned and swung away from her, moving to one of the cane chairs and dropping into it. He waved Bethany to another chair. 'You may sit.'

She sank on to the cushions with almost sagging relief. She hated feeling weak and stupid, and was very grateful to have the table separating her from the man who had reduced her to such...such malleable putty. It was worse than tyrannical. She could fight tyranny, or manoeuvre around it. But the personal effect he had on her was beyond the bounds of reason, and it wasn't fair at all.

'At the airport...' he mused, 'I felt then that you were no ordinary woman. You stood out...but it was more than your singular beauty. You affected me...'

Bethany instantly felt better. There wasn't quite the same imbalance as she had first thought. If he considered her beautiful, if he found her attractive...a few feminine wiles might secure lenient treatment.

His eyes narrowed. 'Let us measure the depth of your power,' he said, uncannily echoing her own private calculating. 'How did you convince P.J. Weatherly to help you in this rash adventure?'

The soft question tripped Bethany's conscience again. First Abdul, now P.J.—she could not let either of them be blamed for her misadventures. She threw a resentful glare at her relentless inquisitor, then heaved a resigned sigh. His relaxed figure projected the air that he had all the time in the world to draw the truth from her.

She had been caught out, well and truly, and any more evasions would only waste time that was precious to her; if, of course, by some miracle, Prince Zakr decided to let her go.

The whole truth, Bethany decided, except for the whisky. Owning up to the bottle of Johnny Walker *Swing* might really be asking for trouble.

With her face set in stubborn defiance, she reeled off all the salient facts: excusing P.J., excusing Abdul, and inadvertently revealing far too much about herself in proving that she had not harebrained off into the desert without a great deal of forethought and planning.

She had only just finished speaking when the tent-flap was opened and a man came in bearing a tray. The first cup of coffee was served, and Bethany looked down at it suspiciously. Apparently she had to drink three of these, and it looked very thick and black. She eyed the plate of sweet biscuits and sticky *halwa* with more favour. It had been a long time since breakfast and, now that she had been forced into inactivity, she felt very hungry.

The sheikh asked his servant to summon some person whose name was Mohammed.

Prince Zakr made no comment on her story. He simply watched her with unswerving intensity, his fingers joined together under his chin. Bethany could not help worrying over what he wanted Mohammed for, but he did not enlighten her. His servant was dismissed and he turned his attention to the coffee on the table.

At least the cups were small, Bethany consoled herself. She waited until the sheikh lifted his cup, and then took a sip. The thick, black liquid was definitely coffee, but spiced with cloves and something else she could not define. It was unusual but not unpleasant.

The biscuits were absolutely delicious—terribly fattening, but that was the least of Bethany's troubles at the moment. She ate her fill of them, not at all sure when her next meal might be. Or if she would survive the sheikh's displeasure to have another meal at all.

'It is a matter of some puzzlement to me that you have come to this country alone,' he remarked. 'Are there no men in your family who could have escorted you.'

Bethany shook her head. 'I'm an only child. And all my parents' relatives live in Scotland. My mother died when I was sixteen, so you see, I've only got Dad.' Her chin lifted stubbornly. 'And I won't accept that he's dead just because he's missing.'

He ignored her defiance. 'There is no man to whom you could turn for protection?' he persisted.

Bethany sighed. No doubt about it, she had entered a man's world...with a vengeance. 'No, there's not,' she replied patiently.

He nodded, as if satisfied with her answer. 'You will not find your father in the Jebel Hafit mountains, Bethany.'

His soft use of her first name surprised her. It sounded friendly, and her heart leapt with pleasure and relief. He wasn't angry any more. Unless this was a new ploy to get her off guard, her mind instantly cautioned. This man was too dangerous to take lightly.

'I didn't expect to find him there,' she answered with complete honesty.

'Then why go?'

Bethany considered the question for several moments before deciding that honesty was still the best policy. 'I thought he might have left a clue behind. My father is the most resourceful man in the world. He knew I would come after him; and if there was any chance at all, he would have done something to indicate what had happened to him. It's just a matter of knowing how to look,' she said with passionate conviction. If she could convince him...

He shook his head. 'There was nothing. I sympathise with your natural grief, but this sentimental journey would only have yielded you disappointment. It is better that you accept that your father is dead. And I do not say that lightly.'

Bethany's mind closed like a steel trap, instantly rejecting his words. 'Did you know my father personally?'

'He was introduced to me. A dedicated scholar. I regret his loss. Such men are rare.'

'Yes,' said Bethany, snatching up the point. 'And not to be underestimated.'

He nodded, but his next words dispelled Bethany's hope that she could change his judgement. 'The love you bear your father does him honour. And so it should be. But when a man knowingly puts his life at risk, he does not expect, nor would he want his daughter to come after him. The only consolation in death is in leaving an heir to carry on the blood-line. And that is your responsibility, Bethany, since your father has no son.'

Bethany sighed in frustration. This man could never understand the kind of relationship she shared with her father. 'He would have come after me if I'd been missing,' she muttered.

'It is not the same,' he murmured.

A soldier entered the tent, diverting the dark gaze from her. The sheikh gave him an order in Arabic which sparked Bethany's full attention.

'What did you tell him to put on my jeep?' she demanded as soon as the soldier had withdrawn.

For the first time, she saw surprise flit over the austere features of her adversary. 'You speak Arabic?'

'Some,' she admitted reluctantly, feeling she was giving away an advantage.

He smiled, and Bethany felt a curious lurch in her heart. Somehow the smile transformed his face, making it look devilishly attractive. And much, much younger. She hadn't tried to place his age before, but she suddenly realised, with a shock, that he couldn't be much older than thirty. Maybe thirty-five, she revised, as the smile faded. Possibly forty, she frowned, thinking of the absolute authority he wielded.

'It is of no consequence. I merely wanted to ensure that your jeep will take you safely back to al-'Ayn,' he replied carelessly.

Bethany latched on to the words in breathless hope. 'You are letting me go?'

His reply was delayed by the serving of the second cup of coffee. Bethany gulped it down impatiently, her big blue eyes fixed imploringly on the sheikh. He gave her his half-smile that she found so impossible to read.

'I must be feeling more tolerant than usual today,' he remarked. 'Perhaps your beauty...your appeal...makes me more forgiving. And I appreciate that you have different ways and customs from my people. I hope you will appreciate that we conduct our lives along more fundamental lines. I will not have you doing any more foolish and dangerous things. You will be safe at al-'Ayn. If you promise me you will go back there, I shall let you go.'

'I promise,' she said earnestly, barely holding back a grin of pure relief. However foolish and dangerous it might be to go on to the mountains, Bethany knew she had no other choice. Neither P.J. or Prince Zakr believed her father to be alive. This was her only chance to prove otherwise, and she would stoop to any trickery to achieve that purpose.

'Straight back!' he insisted.

Which was a slightly more difficult promise to deal with.

'Well, I can't guarantee driving straight across the desert,' she said cautiously. 'I'm sure I bypassed a *sabakha* on the way here. I might deviate just a fraction. I'm not very experienced at using the compass, but I'm sure I can get back to al-'Ayn eventually.'

After she had looked through the caves in the Jebel Hafit mountains!

He looked hard at her, and Bethany had the very uncomfortable impression that he had just read her mind. 'Don't think you can fool me, Bethany,' he warned her quietly. 'From now on I will follow your movements and be aware of where you are all the time. If you do not obey my wishes...' he paused to lend more impact to his next words '...I will discipline you myself. And don't expect me to be tolerant a second time. Even if you are beautiful.'

'It's very good of you to take such a personal interest in me,' Bethany soothed with a wide-eyed look of limpid innocence. 'But really, there is no need. I am used to looking after myself.'

He ignored her protest. 'Wait at al-'Ayn for me. I will see that you are allowed to examine the official reports concerning your father. Perhaps then you will accept the inevitable verdict.'

Never, she silently vowed, but she constructed a grateful smile. 'Thank you. You're most kind.'

'I also wish to see you... when your mind is at peace.'

Bethany felt it was highly unlikely that she could ever be at peace in *his* company. Two meetings with him had proved that to her. He was a very disturbing person. And he held views that she couldn't agree with at all. But she would face that problem when she came to it, if she ever did. Her best policy now was to keep everything smooth and polite, so she smiled and said, 'I'll look forward to it.'

The third cup of coffee was brought in, and Bethany downed it with such speed that it barely touched her throat. 'May I go now?' she asked. 'I really didn't mean to interrupt your hunting, and I'm very, very sorry for holding you up so long.'

He stood, tall and commanding, and totally unnerving as he moved over to Bethany and gently
brushed her fringe away from her eyes. 'While you
re-pin your hair and replace your hat, I shall order
an escort for you.'

'An escort?' Bethany struggled to hide her
dismay. 'I'm sure I don't need one of those, and it
would make me feel really mean about taking your
men away from their...their sport. Please don't...'

'It is to preserve our sport that I will have you
escorted to the edge of the hunting grounds. You
will trespass no further.'

'Oh! Yes, of course. Thank you,' she said jerkily.
His close presence was creating confusion in her
mind again, not to mention playing havoc with her
pulse-rate. Could he see the fear in her eyes? She
desperately wished he would move away.

'Don't make any more trouble for me, Bethany,'
he said in that soft voice that seemed to squeeze
her heart.

'I'll try very hard not to,' she averred, and meant
every word. For the rest of today she would do her
level best to avoid him.

He searched her eyes for a moment longer,
causing ripples of panic in her stomach, then, to
her great relief, he turned away and walked out of
the tent. Bethany's hands were trembling so much,
she made a terrible hash of pinning up her hair,
but she crammed her hat over it and managed to
tuck up the dangling ends.

She remembered his comment about sunglasses,
and whipped them out of her top pocket where she
had tucked them for handy reach. It was only sen-

sible to put them on now anyway, and they gave her a more armoured feeling against the men she had to face outside.

When she emerged from the tent, the sheikh was talking to Mohammed, who was nodding in affirmation. A number of mounted soldiers were waiting near the jeep, and another soldier was seated behind the wheel.

The sheikh escorted Bethany to the passenger seat and handed her in.

There was no sign of merriment from the men now, and Bethany realised that she had just received a singular honour that afforded her great respect. 'Thank you so much,' she murmured with real gratitude.

His face was redrawn into its austere pattern of authority. 'Al-'Ayn,' he reminded her sternly.

'Al-'Ayn,' she repeated solemnly, as if it were a religious vow. And she would keep to it, too... in her own good time.

Unfortunately, she didn't think Prince Zakr Tahnun Sadiq would understand that reasoning very easily. But she had to go on to the Jebel Hafit mountains. Official reports would be of no help whatsoever. The sheikh meant her well. She was almost sure he did. But he was altogether too autocratic about her father's death. Too autocratic about everything.

No one here was going to take any notice of what she believed. No one else knew her father as well as she did, and, unless she came up with some evidence that would raise a reasonable doubt about his supposed death, no one would do anything. She had to find that evidence. Her father's life depended on it.

The sheikh hadn't made her promise *not* to go to the Jebel Hafit mountains. Only to go back to al-'Ayn. And, of course, she would do precisely that, but at her own convenience.

CHAPTER FOUR

THEY took her back to the other side of what Bethany had rightly recognised as a *sabakha*. The soldier who had driven the jeep gave precise instructions on how best to find her way to the oasis. It was a relatively simple matter if she followed his directions.

'How far do the hunting grounds extend?' she asked cautiously. The last thing she wanted was to trespass on them again, thereby risking another encounter with the sheikh.

'Many miles,' was the indeterminate answer.

'But am I at the boundary now?' Bethany persisted.

'One boundary,' he agreed.

Bethany smiled. 'Thank you very much.'

He gave her a respectful bow, then mounted the horse that had been brought along for him. The whole escort lined up like a cavalry guard of honour to watch her depart.

There seemed to be a need for some form of protocol so she gave them all the equivalent of a royal wave as she drove off.

Bethany kept a check on them in the rear-vision mirror. Not a horse even twitched while she was in sight. She fiercely hoped they would all turn back once she was lost to view. Bethany didn't risk

stopping for ten miles, and by that time she was
fairly certain that she hadn't been followed.

Meanwhile her mind had been very busy re-
assessing her meeting with the sheikh. Somehow it
seemed out of character for him to let her drive
back to al-'Ayn alone. Why hadn't he ordered at
least one soldier to take her all the way? She had
the eerie feeling that he was testing her, that
somehow he had a control that would leap out and
snap around her if she dared to deviate from his
demands.

It disturbed her. But then the man himself had
disturbed her to such an extent that she wasn't sure
if she was thinking rationally any more. Maybe her
feverish imagination was granting him super-powers
that simply didn't exist. Yet intuition had never
steered her wrong before. On the other hand, his
men were gone . . . how could he possibly know if
she took a little detour on her way back to al-'Ayn?

She got out her map and relocated herself on it.
Quite a big detour, in actual fact. She would have
to make a huge semicircular sweep through the
desert if she was to avoid any possibility of en-
countering Prince Zakr again . . . at least four extra
hours on to her trip.

A check on her watch showed that it was just
past ten o'clock. If she went on, it would mean
most of her return journey would have to be driven
in darkness, which was a rather daunting prop-
osition. However, if she didn't go on, she would
never again get another opportunity to search
through the caves.

Once she was back in al-'Ayn, Abdul would undoubtedly stick to her like a leech. P.J. was probably alarmed about her right now, and certainly wouldn't countenance her taking the jeep again. So what choice did she have? None! Despite her forebodings, she had to carry on.

Bethany started up the jeep again and drove with steadfast purpose, keeping careful checks on her odometer and compass at every change in direction.

The sun climbed higher. The hours of monotonous driving passed slowly. Heat rose from the desert in shimmering waves. But she was closing back towards the mountains now, and the end was in sight.

The atmosphere became thick and more oppressive as she got nearer to her destination. It reminded Bethany of the heavy stillness in the air before a thunderstorm at home; but there were no clouds in the sky, and it didn't rain in the desert, anyway. She shrugged off the feeling. One more sand dune and the caves would surely be in view!

Her gaze was trained on the mountain-face as the jeep crested the dune, but she caught the flash of red and blue out of the corner of her eye. Her head instantly swivelled and her heart slammed around her chest as the rider swept down the adjoining dune on an intersecting course with her jeep.

The white Arab stallion was at full gallop, a magnificent beast, the plume of its tail held high, its mane streaming with exultant speed; but the control exerted by its rider was patently evident when the horse was reined back to a plunging halt directly in Bethany's path. She didn't need any second glance to identify her nemesis.

Prince Zakr Tahnun Sadiq raised his hand in command. It was quite obvious that he was indicating she should stop.

With a wild rush of blood to the head, Bethany jammed her foot down hard on the accelerator and spun the wheel. She couldn't drive straight at him and hurt either him or the horse, but she was not going to stop now! Not for him or...she threw a frightened glance around... Thank God! There was no one else in sight.

Adrenalin pumped through her body as the jeep swung sideways and then straightened up. Having careered around her would-be captor, she sped off without a care about direction. A mad exhilaration blotted out any sensible thought of consequences. He couldn't catch her! Not on a horse. No way. He couldn't...

A shot rang out and the jeep slewed sideways as one of the back tyres lost its adhesion. A petrifying bolt of fear kept Bethany's foot on the accelerator as she wrestled frantically with the wheel. If she could only get far enough away she could change the tyre. The jeep carried a spare.

A second shot rang out. The jeep dragged to a halt, both back tyres spinning uselessly in the sand. Bethany banged the wheel in sheer frustration. There was no way she could get away now!

Frustration seethed into anger. He might have wounded her with one of those shots! Even killed her! Didn't he have any respect for human life? Didn't he realise he had just wrecked her only means of transport? The man was worse than a fanatic! He was a maniac!

Tears blurred her eyes. She whipped off her sunglasses and rubbed away the revealing moisture. He was not going to find her crying. Nor would she cower to him or look beaten in any way. Damn him! Damn him to hell for interfering in what was none of his business!

She jumped out of the jeep and strode back to look at the damage, her eyes raging fury at the rider who was calmly sliding a rifle back into some kind of saddle holster. The tyres were blown to ribbons.

Bethany raised a fist in shaking defiance as Prince Zakr rode towards her. 'You...you...' All her frustrations tumbled into one screaming demand. 'How did you find me?'

One twist of the reins and the mighty white stallion stood absolutely still. Its master remained in the saddle, his face carved in scornful disdain, his eyes glittering down at Bethany with cold black savagery.

'There was not one moment when I didn't know where you were. A tracking device was attached to your jeep while you were in my tent, even as you gave me your promise to go straight back to al-'Ayn.'

Her jeep had been bugged! Letting her go *had* been a trap, just as her intuition had warned her, and she had been driving around in a circle for nothing. Bethany glared up at the man who had outwitted her. 'Of all the tricky, underhanded...'

'Apply those terms to yourself. I needed to know exactly what you are...to test you. You have failed.

I cannot get you to be sensible. Therefore you will be given no choice in the matter from now on. You will learn to obey me, Bethany Lyon McGregor. I warned you I would not be tolerant a second time.'

'Tolerant!' she shrieked. 'You could have shot me while you were popping off that damned rifle!'

'A great hunter does not miss his target. I am not called "The Falcon" for nothing. And I have other uses for your body.'

'You . . . what?' Bethany almost swallowed her tongue as his last words penetrated the haze of rage that had kept her fighting even after she had recognised the helplessness of her position.

'You have challenged me as a man, and now you will know me as a man. I will never let you go again. It is unfortunate for your independent spirit that you have kindled in me a desire that only you can appease . . .'

As Bethany stood there, open-mouthed with shock, he spurred his horse forward, leaned over, and scooped her off her feet.

'Put me down!' she screeched as she was lifted on to his lap.

He ignored her, pinning her against him with one iron-tight arm while he hoisted her leg over the saddle. Then he flicked the reins and the horse pranced off into a gallop. The enforced contact with the very male body behind her was electrifying. Bethany panicked, clawing at his arm and kicking her feet back at him.

'You can't get away with this! I'll fight you to the very end!'

'Be still!' he rasped in her ear. 'If you fall, you'll get hurt, and there's no time to waste. The *kaus* will be on us in a few minutes.'

His arm was holding her so tightly that she could barely breathe, and the urgency in his voice fractured the scream in her head with another fear. 'Who are the *kaus*?' she gasped.

His voice was a whip of contempt. 'You think I would run from anything human? It is only the forces of nature that I acknowledge as my master. The *kaus* is the seasonal sandstorm that will flail all the beautiful white skin from your body unless I get us to shelter in time.'

Sand! How much sand got blown about in a *kaus*? The medical supplies! 'All my things in the jeep...'

'I'll have them recovered for you later. We must reach the empty caves of the Shihuh before the storm reaches us.'

The caves of the Shihuh! It was where she had wanted to go! Bethany stopped straining against his hold and sank back against him, instinctively seeking all the protection he would give her from the impending storm.

The initial sense of comfort in his warmth and strength was very brief. The constant friction of their bodies moving to the rhythm of the galloping horse produced the most uncomfortable sensations Bethany had ever experienced.

Her awareness of his masculinity was heightened in a terribly intimate fashion with every stride. Then there were his thighs pressing hard against hers; the arm across her diaphragm, just under the swell of her breasts; the warm fan of his breath on her skin.

Her hat had been knocked off in the lift on to the horse, and she realised his face was close to hers so as not to have his vision obscured by flying locks of hair, but she even found herself waiting for...wanting...the occasional rub of his cheek against hers.

Bethany was half appalled by what she was feeling, but she could not deny the physical fascination in every contact. It disturbed her deeply. All her life she had been in control of herself...in control of whatever she was doing and saying and feeling. But things were happening to her now that she couldn't account for.

The confusing reactions that Prince Zakr had drawn from her when he had touched her in his tent were nothing to what he was arousing in her now. Her heart was thundering with excitement. A sweet ache was spreading through her stomach. Her thighs were quivering jelly. And she knew that the heat that was suffusing through her had nothing to do with the desert sun. He was doing this to her. And he wasn't really doing anything!

She had been held by men before, but never to such devastating effect. And she had been a nurse too long for there to be any mysteries about a male body. Why should the hard flesh and muscle pressed so close to her now be any different? He had threatened that he would never let her go, and Bethany was even entertaining the thought that she didn't want him to anyway. And what kind of mad thought was that when she still had to find her father?

Nevertheless, she felt curiously bereft when he slowed the horse to a halt and dismounted. They had reached the foot of the mountains and there were steep, stony paths leading up to caves in the cliff-face.

He lifted her down from the horse and for a moment his hands lingered on her waist, steadying her, feeling the light, nimble strength under his hands. 'Now you obey me,' he breathed, his eyes raking hers with fierce satisfaction. 'Go up to the first cave. I will lead my horse up behind you.'

He gave her a little push towards the path, and Bethany half stumbled forward. Her legs were alarmingly shaky, but she forced them into action, all too aware of the man following closely on her footsteps. And aware that the sky had darkened.

Bethany tottered into the cave. Prince Zakr grabbed her hand and pulled her with him as far as the cave extended inside the cliff, which was not very far. About fifteen yards, Bethany estimated, but she didn't like the oppressive feeling of the rock-face closing in around her. Better than the sand-storm, she consoled herself, and tried not to think about what other dangers she faced with the man who had brought her here.

He released her hand and attended to his horse. She watched, shivering a little in apprehension as he removed the saddle-cloth and draped it over the horse's head, tying it down so that it couldn't be shaken off.

Would the sand blow all the way in here? Her eyes darted to the cave opening, and the realisation suddenly burst on her that she had actually reached her planned destination.

'This is where my father was?' she asked, wanting absolute confirmation.

'Yes. In such a place as this,' he answered. 'Look around you. He had to be a dedicated scholar to put up with such conditions, even with regular supplies to sustain him. He had a great thirst for knowledge. An extraordinary man.' He swung around to face her, his eyes too dark to read. 'This country will miss him greatly.'

'He's alive, I tell you,' Bethany hurled back at him, her emotions churning against the all too obvious implication of his words. 'And somehow I'll find him!'

He shook his head and walked slowly towards her, each step a menacing encroachment on her resistance to all he stood for. 'Do not grieve for the impossible,' he said in a softer, more sympathetic tone. 'I will look after you . . . be more to you than a father.'

'You can't!' she cried. 'And if the positions were reversed, my father would never give up.'

He lifted his hands and cupped her face. 'You might have the courage of a man, Bethany, but you must be taught you are a woman. And I can . . . and will . . . mean more to you than anyone else ever could.'

His fingers raked back through her hair and he held her head tilted up to his; Bethany was defenceless to the hungry assault of his mouth. The rapacious intimacy of his kiss left her weak and gasping and totally devastated. There was no fight left in her at all as his arms swept her against him. Shivery sensations were erupting through her body, and she literally sagged into his warmth and strength, needing his support.

His mouth moved warmly over her temples. 'Do not be afraid. I will protect you,' he murmured, and there was no longer any cold steel in his voice. It was a soft, seductive murmur that breathed tingling life into her skin.

Bethany didn't doubt that he would protect her from the storm outside, but who was going to protect her from the storm inside her own body...the storm of sensation that was rioting through her?

Even her normally strong will-power was playing traitor to any sense of morality. She didn't want to move. Yet she couldn't just surrender to what he was doing to her. She tried to reason a way out of it, but her mind was not co-operating at all.

It was he who moved, gently easing her out of his embrace. Bethany stared up at him, her heart quivering in helpless indecision. His hands started to unzip and part her battle-jacket.

'No...please...you can't!' Bethany gasped, her own hands scrabbling at his in agitated protest. It was one thing to feel sexual desire, quite another to be undressed by a man she barely knew.

'The sand will start flying in here any minute now. It's best that we lie down. You can put this under your head.'

'Oh!' Embarrassed heat flooded her cheeks. Feeling hopelessly foolish about the assumption she had made, Bethany stopped resisting and let him take the jacket off.

He felt the hardness in its bottom pocket as he spread it on the sandy floor. 'What have you here?' he demanded sharply.

'A...a torch. To search the caves.' God! She couldn't even speak firmly!

He took out the torch and laid it aside. Then he straightened up and stared down at her for several long, nerve-stretching moments. The grave, considering concentration of his eyes on her did dreadful things to the pit of Bethany's stomach.

His hand slowly lifted and slid under her hair to the nape of her neck. His thumb found and caressed a sensitive area just behind her ear. He stepped forward. Bethany drew a quick breath, but he hadn't moved to kiss her again.

He picked her up in his arms, cradling her tightly against his chest for a moment, then lowered her to the floor of the cave. Very gently he laid her head on the spread jacket, then paused to stroke her hair back from her ears, suggesting a tenderness that mixed oddly with the way he had invaded her mouth.

He stood over her, his arms lifted to stretch out his cloak, and in the dim light of the cave, his dark silhouette was forcefully that of a bird of prey...a great falcon about to swoop.

The same fear she had felt at Rhafhar airport came rushing back...the fear of his power to control her, change her into something other than she had been. Already she was almost unrecognisable to herself. Yet there seemed to be nothing she could do about it.

Every nerve in her body was tingling with anticipation, wanting whatever he would do to her, and as he knelt and covered her with his body, his cloak enclosing them both in a dark, private world of their own, a shudder of wholly primitive satisfaction rippled through her.

He eased some of his weight aside, his hand stroking down her body in a gentle affirmation that she was his to touch as he willed, and just that one possessive caress set Bethany trembling. His lips grazed slowly over her face, as if savouring the taste or texture of her skin, and she did not move. She did nothing at all to stop him. She felt caught in a sensual thrall that she was powerless to resist.

She heard the hiss of flying sand, heard the distressed whinny of the horse and its restless movements under the sting of the storm; but the wild thumping of her heart was much louder.

His lips reached hers, their pressure tantalisingly gentle, persuasive, seductive. He forced nothing from her, yet Bethany could not stop herself from inviting the warm invasion of his mouth, submitting willingly, eagerly, to his searching possession; tentatively carrying out a search of her own as the erotic intimacy flooded her with pulsating sensations.

He withdrew, sweeping her lips with his in a tender salute to her response. 'You have never had a lover, Bethany?' he asked, so softly that she only just caught the words.

She found it difficult to speak. Her tongue was still furred with the tingling taste of his. 'Not...like you,' she whispered.

'You have never been with a man?'

His voice held a distant reserve, as if he was determining something that he had not put into words.

What answer did he want? Bethany's sense of self-preservation hastily rephrased that thought... what answer was best for her?

If she admitted to being a virgin, would he respect her chastity, or take more pleasure in being the first to possess her? If she confessed to a string of lovers, would he use her carelessly, or decide she wasn't worth having?

'The truth, Bethany,' he commanded, as if he clearly read the hesitation in her mind. 'You will be mine, anyway. I have decided that. It will not alter anything, but you will rue the lie if you try to deceive me.'

The inevitability of her fate was sealed...and however much Bethany's dazed mind struggled against it...there was an insidious attraction about that inevitability. He meant to bend her to his will and already he was making her compliant.

There was something about this man that she couldn't fight. Even at the airport at Rhafhar...when he had looked at her, touched her...and in his tent today...and now with his body pressed so close...stirring a wanting, a need that only he had ever aroused...

It was too much to fight. And what could she do, anyway? He was far stronger than her. Even if she managed to force her way free of him, what escape was there with a sandstorm raging outside the cave?

'Tell me.'

The soft insistence brought a well of sadness. Whenever she had thought of how it would be, it was always with love. She did not even know if she liked Prince Zakr, yet he pulled at some essential core of her being in a way she was sure no other man would. She wished...

Tears brimmed her eyes and trickled out of the corners as she gave him the truth. 'No, I've never had a lover.'

He rubbed his cheek gently against hers, and felt the little rivulet of moisture. He lifted his head and pressed feather-soft kisses to her eyelids. 'Do not weep. It will be as you have dreamed. That I promise you. I shall ravish all your senses. You will forget everything else but me.'

'No...' she moaned in sinking desperation. She couldn't forget everything else. She had come to find her father. Somewhere in this desert land he was in need, and she couldn't forget him. Ever!

But, oh, God! she melted as he licked the tears from her face. 'Do not weep,' he repeated softly. 'I am not without feeling for you.'

'You are! You must be!' she cried, jerking her head aside from the seductive tenderness of his kisses. 'I'm not...just something...you can take,' she gasped out in a tortured denial of what he was doing to her.

'It was written when I first saw you,' he said in a soft, compelling voice that swept aside any argument she might raise. 'And everything I've learnt about you since then confirms it. Why do you argue against what you know to be true? You are drawn to me as I am drawn to you.'

Bethany couldn't, in all truth, deny those last words when her whole body was pulsing in wanton response to his. A terrible uncertainty was slicing through her mind, robbing her of any determination.

He gently turned her face back to his. *'I have decided!'*

And he kissed her with an intense passion that demonstrated all too clearly that he could do anything he wished with her. Bethany could not prevent herself from succumbing to it. And with her helpless submission came the feeling that she would never be a whole single-minded person, ever again.

CHAPTER FIVE

BETHANY had no idea how long the sandstorm lasted. She had forgotten it. What was happening to her underneath Prince Zakr's cloak was the only reality...a pulsing, vivid reality that had swept her beyond the borders of reason.

She had no sense of time. Every moment held a life of its own as Zakr stroked her quivering body with a gentle, knowing touch, each kiss and caress swelling a tide of compelling need that craved fulfilment. Bethany felt ready to explode with excitement when, unaccountably, he ceased all movement.

He lifted his head and brushed his lips over hers, stifling the moan of protest that whispered from her throat. 'It has stopped,' he murmured. 'Listen to the silence.'

Bethany couldn't listen. Every nerve-end in her body was screaming for him to complete what he had started. How could he be aware of anything else? she cried in silent frustration. And she knew then . . . she knew that it was only she who was out of control. He was her master in this, as he had been in everything else. She shuddered in sheer misery at her helpless vulnerability to this man.

He bent and kissed her lips with a slow sensuality that did nothing to soothe the turmoil inside her. 'I hurt, too,' he murmured. 'But this comfortless

77

place is not appropriate for your first time, Bethany. Tonight we will have all the time we need to sate our every desire in the way it should be done.'

'Zakr . . .' It was a half-choked sigh. Bethany did not quite know what to say. Sanity screamed that she should not submit to his plans for tonight, yet everything within her yearned to know the intimacy he promised.

He kissed her again. A brief, whimsical kiss. 'I like my name on your lips.'

She could hear the smile in his voice, and wondered if he felt any more than a passing desire for her.

'We must leave. The *kaus* has passed over, yet even with me it is too dangerous for you to stay here.'

He lifted off the protective cloak as he pulled himself to his feet. Bethany felt too weak to move, but when he stared down at her, an uncharacteristic self-consciousness drove her to her feet. She swayed, her legs almost giving way under her, and he caught her to him in a quick, fiercely possessive embrace.

'You are as beautiful as I wanted you to be.'

He spoke as if he was the only person in the world that she had to please. And perhaps he was, Bethany thought in light-headed hysteria. How could there be any other man after this?

Having steadied her on her feet, he picked up her jacket, shook it free of sand, held it while she thrust her arms into the sleeves, then zipped it up for her. When he left her in order to attend to his horse, Bethany stared after him, dazed by the realisation that her life had been inexorably changed by this man's will.

'What are you going to do?' she asked, her mind strangely numb, incapable of working out anything.

'I have a miniature two-way radio with me. I will have a helicopter sent to pick us up.'

Bethany watched him open a small saddle-bag and remove the very modern piece of technology. Her brain ticked over sluggishly. Of course, he had needed that for tracking the jeep.

'P.J.'s jeep!' she gasped in guilt-stricken horror. 'We can't leave it in the desert for someone to steal. And your horse...'

'I will have men flown in to attend to those trivial matters.' He turned to her, no longer the man who had held her in his arms, but the autocratic Sheikh of Bayrar, in total command of the situation. 'Come! We will go outside and make the call.'

Bethany's foot kicked something that made a metallic sound as it rolled. The torch! She swiftly bent and picked it up before following Prince Zakr out of the cave. It forcefully reminded her of why she had come to the Jebel Hafit mountains.

She didn't really mean anything to Zakr, she thought despairingly. How could she? She was from another world. Another culture. She was just a body he wanted to find pleasure with. Only her father loved her, and now she was going to let him down. Unless...

She squared her shoulders, intent on fighting Zakr's insidious influence on her. She had to make a stand for her father's sake, and her own. 'Zakr, I'm going to look through the caves while you make your call,' she stated with desperate determination. 'You cannot...must not refuse me,' she added, silently begging him to understand and not forbid her this one chance.

He looked hard at her for a moment, then slowly nodded. 'Very well.'

'Thank you,' she breathed, grateful for the un-expected concession.

His mouth gave that half-curl that could have meant anything, but Bethany did not waste time trying to interpret it.

The caves deeply depressed her. Not only were they empty of all signs of habitation, just as P.J. had told her, but she could not even imagine how anyone had lived in them. They were so...so barren of comfort...oppressive...yet it was in places like these that primitive man had lived. Still lived. The Shihuh were not a myth.

Her father had been fascinated that a tribe of blue-eyed people existed in a land where the rest of mankind was dark-eyed. Where had they come from? How had they survived? Did they still survive? Bethany asked herself. Despair crept into her heart; had they been wiped out...along with her father?

Tears blurred her eyes. Was her father really dead, as Zakr insisted? The words he had spoken at Rhafhar beat through her mind like drums of doom. 'This country is not like your own...when the lifeline of communication is discontinued...'

There had not been even a scrap of paper in the caves she had searched. No communication. This was the last cave, and there had been nothing in any of them to give her the slightest thread of hope. Bethany heaved a defeated sigh and listlessly shone the torch in a sweep around the back of the cave before she finally gave up.

The beam of light caught the edge of a charcoal drawing. The communication of a primitive man, Bethany thought with an ironic twist, but a flicker of interest drew her forward to examine the drawing more closely. A crescent moon, she decided, and what looked like a rudely executed hammer. She moved the torch beam lower.

Her heart stopped dead, then pounded in wild triumph as the printed words leapt out at her. Only her father's hand could have written them, just as he had done so on the front pages of her textbooks after he had written her name in them when she was a little girl. With tears in her eyes and a bubble of laughter in her voice, she recited them out loud— 'S'rioghal mo dhream.'

How often had he recited that Gaelic phrase to her in pride and encouragement! Bethany had heard it all her life, almost from the moment she had been born to her parents in the upper reaches of the Amazon River. Her father's scholarly dedication insisted that she be taught some Gaelic, and certainly the long history of the McGregor clan.

His blood had been well and truly fired with life when he had written this, Bethany thought with fierce satisfaction. But what did the drawings mean? They had to convey some pertinent message. She studied them again, trying to see them through her father's academic mind.

'Bethany!'

She did not even hear the curt impatience with which he spoke her name. In sheer exultation, she almost danced down the cave to where Zakr stood just inside the entrance.

'I've found him! I've found my father!' she cried excitedly. 'Come and see! I'll show you.'

He accompanied her without comment until it was obvious that the cave was unoccupied. 'I don't see anyone here,' he growled.

'But he was here!' Bethany protested, ignoring the displeasure in his tone. She shone the torch on the wall, picking up the drawings and the printing. 'He left this message, telling where he's gone.'

He frowned. 'This is meaningless. Neither English nor Arabic.'

'It's Gaelic. The McGregor clan comes from Scotland and this is their motto...' she threw him a happy grin '...or their battle-cry. *S'rioghal mo dhream*,' she repeated proudly.

Zakr was still frowning. 'What does it mean?'

'Royal is my blood,' she translated for him.

'You are of royal blood?'

'Of course,' Bethany replied carelessly, more anxious to get on with finding her father than having a discourse on her genealogy. She did not see the flash of understanding, nor the satisfaction that settled in Zakr's dark eyes.

'Now look at the drawings,' she rushed on, pinpointing them with the torch. 'See the hammer? And this crescent moon...if you add a straight line at the bottom of it, it becomes a sickle. A hammer and sickle, Zakr! It must have been the Marxist guerrillas from the Yemen who took my father away. Obviously he couldn't write something they could read, but he knew I'd come looking for him. He knew...'

'It changes nothing, Bethany.' His voice was hard and cold, with a calculated ring of finality.

It shocked her out of her elation. Her voice climbed in vehement argument against his rigid stance. 'Of course it does! A dead man didn't write that! And you can't believe that it could have been anyone else except my father. That's the proof I came to find. The evidence that...'

'The evidence that one of the possibilities I listed is now a certainty. The Marxist guerrillas don't take prisoners.'

'You don't know that for a certainty!' she cried, clinging obsessively to her own belief that had been re-nurtured in this cave. 'They sometimes take hostages, don't they?'

'There has been no demand,' he stated with inexorable logic.

It hurt. It hurt so much that Bethany flew out of control. 'I don't care! I don't care what you say!' she yelled at him in her anguish. 'He's alive. I know he is. And if you won't do anything about it, I'll find him myself!'

'You will not!'

'I will so! You can't stop me! I'll get away from you and...'

He stepped forward and caught her flailing arms, forcing them down and pinning them to her side. She glared up at him, heaving with rebellion, yet weakened by the authority his formidable presence exerted over her.

'Now listen to me, Bethany Lyon McGregor. I know you wish to go charging off into the desert, into the unknown on your holy quest. I see it written in the deep blue wells of your eyes. But it will not be so. You will stay with me, where I can keep you under surveillance all the time. It is for your own good.'

She bit down on her quivering lower lip. He didn't understand, and she had already been blindly reckless in defying him. She felt like crying. Why wouldn't he help her? Why? Couldn't he give . . . as well as take?

'Bethany . . .' It was a sigh of exasperation. 'That inscription on the wall was not written yesterday. It is at least two months old. There is not even any certainty that it was written at the time of your father's disappearance. However, I will notify the proper authorities of its existence.'

He meant his men, Bethany thought in bitter defeat, and his men would no more believe her father was alive than Zakr himself did. He was merely paying lip service to her need, and Bethany despaired of ever winning him over to her point of view.

Perhaps he really was right and there was no hope that her father was still alive.

Even as she anguished over the question, the realisation came to her that she had lost her independence in this man's arms. She had to get away from him before he completely sapped her will. Somewhere there had to be someone who could help her. If she got to P.J. Weatherly with this proof . . .

Zakr's fingertips brushed over her forehead. 'I will not give you the chance, Bethany.'

'What... what do you mean?' she stammered, disconcerted by what had seemed an answer to her thoughts. Could he really read her mind?

The distinctive sound of an approaching helicopter broke into the tense silence between them. 'It is time to go,' Zakr murmured, and the softness of his voice was not unkind.

He took Bethany's hand and led her outside. She went meekly, pulled along by his domination in one sense, but also recognising that this was not the time nor the place to make a stand. It was better for her to appear compliant, not only to Zakr, but to all his people, so that they would think she was doing precisely what the sheikh required of her.

Zakr's control over her was not absolute, Bethany argued determinedly to herself. He could not always be at her side...holding her...touching her... She wrenched her mind off those thoughts and started making resolutions.

At the first opportunity, she would make a run for it. Get back to al-'Ayn and see P.J. And there was the consul, the embassy...the United Nations...she would keep stirring up trouble until something was done!

The helicopter landed near the foot of the cliff-path and an Arab emerged from it, lifting out a large water container. He glanced up at his sheikh, who made a hand signal to him. The man hoisted the container on to his shoulder and hurried up the path. When he arrived at the top, Zakr spoke in rapid Arabic, telling him where the horse was and giving instructions as to its care.

'What about my jeep?' Bethany asked, as Zakr started leading her down the path.

'It is being attended to,' he answered briefly, his autocratic manner in full force.

Bethany refused to be deterred. 'When will I get it back? I have to...'

He sliced her a quelling look. 'You won't be getting it back at all. You have no need for it. It will be returned to P.J. Weatherly, who not only owns it, but whose need far exceeds yours.'

'Of course,' said Bethany, unabashed. 'That's what I had in mind all the time.'

The look in the coal-black eyes warned her that he would never underestimate her again.

'You did promise I would get my things back from the jeep,' she added anxiously. That was imperative if her father was in need of medical help.

'They will be returned to you.' The cold steel edged his voice again. 'I never go back on my word, Bethany.'

'No. No, I'm sure you don't,' she sighed, her thoughts winging forward to what he meant to do with her tonight. The memory of her own mindless response to him sent a wave of heat through her body, and when he gripped her waist to lift her up into the helicopter, his hands seemed to burn through her clothes.

Bethany had never ridden in a helicopter before. It was very noisy, but it did provide a fantastic view. Bethany glued her gaze to the panorama below, doing her utmost to ignore the feelings that Zakr's presence beside her could so easily evoke.

The lowering sun was blood-red and covered in a haze from the sandstorm. The sparse vegetation of the savannah grassland over which they flew merged into the Rub' al Khali desert, which swept away as far as the eye could see, the largest uninterrupted sand-desert in the world. It was an awesome sight, a massive testament that nature could be cruel as well as kind.

Survival of the fittest, Bethany mused, remembering her father's edicts on hostile environments. She could understand that such a land as this had bred a man like Zakr Tahnun Sadiq: ruthless, cruel, unforgiving, yet not without kindness . . . a force of nature. Defy him she might, but she could not deny his power when he exerted it.

A huge building came into sight, growing rapidly with each moment of flight. It was at least three or four storeys high, with a tower, and much larger than any hotel Bethany had seen. Smaller buildings were clustered around it, and the complex was surrounded by a high wall. The helicopter hovered over it, then slowly lowered into a clearing surrounded by palm trees.

An Arab raced across the area to open the helicopter door. Zakr stood and climbed out, then helped Bethany down. "Is this your palace?" she asked apprehensively, wondering how on earth she could escape from such a place. Already armed guards were lining up in a kind of guard of honour for their sheikh.

'No. This is my hunting lodge. You will be taken to the palace later. For the present, it is more convenient to have you here, where I can personally see to your safety.'

His grim smile was without any shade of mercy, and Bethany knew she could expect none at his hands.

He led her into a grand reception hall: marble floor, marble pillars, and the ceiling a geometric arrangement of mirrors supported by gilt mouldings. A hunting lodge, Bethany thought incredulously, but she had little time to assimilate her new surroundings. Zakr clapped his hands and servant girls came running from all directions.

He gave his orders sharply, but Bethany managed to catch the import of them. 'Oh, no, you don't!' she said in fierce rejection, forgetting all about her pose of compliance as she turned on him in absolute outrage. There was a point of submission beyond which she utterly refused to go. 'I'll be damned if I'll have these women washing me!'

One eyebrow lifted in surprise. 'Most people need a bath after they have endured the *kaus*.'

'I'm not against a bath,' Bethany flared at him. 'I'll bathe as long as you like. But by myself, thank you.'

The mouth twitched. 'You wish your privacy to remain . . . inviolate?'

Was he mocking her?

'I certainly prefer it that way,' she said heatedly, remembering how he had stared down at her in the cave, and feeling most uncomfortable with the memory.

'Then it shall be done as you will. However...'
The black eyes held relentless purpose. 'I will have
new clothes sent to you. What you are wearing is
unsuitable, and most unbecoming to a beautiful
woman. Anything you want is yours. You may
order what you like. But you will dress as a woman
when I am to see you.'

He paused to see if her rebellion extended to this
edict, but Bethany had been plunged into emotional
turmoil again, all too aware that she was a woman
when she was near him. 'When...how long will
that be?' she choked out, hoping for the longest
possible respite.

His slow smile held a suggestive anticipation that
sent her pulse racing into chaos. 'I think we shall
dine early.'

There would be no escape from him. None at all.
The thought throbbed relentlessly through
Bethany's mind, driving her to try for some post-
ponement. What could she do? 'Zakr...I'm very
tired. It's been a very long day of driving and...'

'Then sleep. It will be my pleasure to wake you
up when I come to you.' He stroked her cheek in
a tender salute. 'And yours also,' he added softly,
his touch powerfully reinforced by the knowing look
in those devilish black eyes.

The weakness draining through Bethany's thighs
was so pervasive that she felt like crumpling on the
spot, when his hand left her face and he turned
away. She had no chance of resisting him. All he
had to do was touch her like that and she might as
well be his slave.

He meant to take her and he would, no matter what she said or did. But she had to try something! Threaten him with the consequences of his actions...she would tell the Australian ambassador...but would that stop him? No, nothing would stop him, Bethany thought with the same sense of inevitability that had swamped all thoughts of resistance in the cave.

'I am the law. I am the justice. I am absolute monarch.' Zakr's statement of his position marched inexorably through her mind. And what appeal could she make that would possibly persuade him to reconsider his decision when he already knew the depth of her response to him?

As tired as she felt, Bethany knew sleep would be impossible. Her body was almost twitching with nervous excitement, and her mind was sifting too many pressing thoughts for it to close down, even for a minute.

And she was hungry. She hadn't eaten anything since the sweet biscuits in Zakr's tent. She wondered what kind of dinner would be provided in his hunting lodge, and hoped the food would not be too foreign. On the other hand, with Zakr looking at her as he had done just now, would she be able to eat anything at all?

The servant girls started urging Bethany to accompany them. She went with them without argument. After all, she had to be bathed and dressed and made fit for their prince. Never mind about what she felt or wanted.

Bethany's emotions were so confused that she felt she didn't know anything any more, but she wished...she wished with all her heart that what Zakr was about to do to her could have been done with love.

CHAPTER SIX

BETHANY had never seen such a huge bathroom, not even in films. The floor was lined with mosaic tiles, and the actual bath itself was bigger than her bedroom at home. Potted palms added their touch of luxury, and the mirrors everywhere made Bethany feel extremely conscious of her body as she undressed.

Wide, shallow steps edged down into the bath so it was possible to sit or lie at the appropriate level. Bethany sat until she had soaped off all the sand and grime of the desert. Jets of air were blown through the water at various points, and when she finally settled into the bath the relaxing feel of the shooting water soothed the aches and pains of her tired muscles.

At her insistence the women had left her alone, but not before supplying her with every possible toilet article. Bethany washed her hair with a shampoo that smelled vaguely of roses. It was good to feel really clean. She lay down in the bath, letting her hair float around her, moving her legs languorously, enjoying the boneless sensation.

Awakened to a sensuality she had not been aware of before, Bethany stroked her hand over her stomach and trailed her fingertips up to her breasts. Her skin reacted sensitively, but there was none of the tense excitement she had felt when Zakr had

touched her...and that was with her clothes on!
She didn't understand her uncontrollable reaction
to him at all. Why was his touch so different from
hers? Or anyone else's, for that matter?

She had gone out with men she liked—men she
knew well—and none of them had evoked such intense, explosive feelings in her. Her emotions had
always been under control, and she was not used
to feeling confused about anything.

A knock on the bathroom door startled her out
of her reflections. Had she been here too long? Was
Zakr on his way to her? Bethany hoisted herself
out of the bath, grabbed one of the huge towels,
and wrapped it around her body.

'Come in,' she called in Arabic.

The women poured back into the bathroom. They
seemed fascinated by her. Her figure was so slim;
her skin was so white; her eyes so large and blue;
her hair...how was it the colour of the sun? One
of them even asked if it was the same colour *down
there*, whereupon they all fell about giggling.

Of course, it didn't take much guessing what she
was here for, with the sheikh having given such
pointed orders about her. The Falcon's mistress...
He had hunted her, caught her, and tonight he
would devour the girl she had been before she had
met him. Bethany shivered, whether from fear or
anticipation she didn't really know.

One of the women offered to blow-dry her hair,
and she gratefully sank down on the chair in front
of a vanity-table, more than willing to be pampered
in this respect.

She felt curiously drained of all strength. Besides, she could see no advantage in fighting Zakr's servants when they were only trying to please her. If she won their esteem, perhaps they would be compliant to her wishes when she could work out what to do... if there was anything that could be done to get herself out of this terrible impasse.

By the time the woman had finished with her hair, it rippled around her face in shining waves. Several very beautiful, caftan-like gowns were brought to her for approval, and Bethany could not deny their strong feminine appeal.

The blue one, she decided. The fabric was a soft, fine silk. The neckline and the bottom edge of the long, flowing sleeves were delicately embroidered with gold and silver thread.

It was a fabulous gown, and Bethany could never have afforded such splendour on her salary. Oil wealth could become very addictive, she thought, feeling herself in danger of being well and truly seduced by the luxury around her.

Strappy gold sandals were fitted for her. She was given a manicure and a pedicure; her nails varnished with a pearly, opal-pink colour. When the women were finally satisfied that Bethany was all properly polished up for their Prince, they urged her to put on the blue dress.

'But I haven't any underclothes,' Bethany protested. Those she had discarded before her bath had been whisked away by one of the women, and none had been so far provided.

Not needed, seemed the consensus of opinion, and Bethany's pleas were staunchly ignored.

Bethany clung grimly on to her bath-towel and ordered the women out.

They pleaded to see her in her dress and, feeling rather mean for distressing them after all their ministrations, Bethany relented. After all, she supposed it wasn't their fault that she wasn't to be given underclothes.

She allowed herself to be led into a bedroom that was heart-stoppingly dominated by a king-size bed piled high with sumptuous cushions. In two corners of the huge room stood elaborately carved screens. Bethany's gown was hung on one of these, and she was invited to make use of the privacy that the screen provided.

The silk was cool and sensuously soft against her bare skin. Bethany was extremely conscious of her braless nipples peaking into prominence against the fabric. She wished the embroidery had extended over her breasts to disguise the fact, but there was nothing she could do about it. She slid her feet into the gold sandals and stepped out from behind the screen.

The little squeals of delight were embarrassing enough, but when the women actually clapped her, Bethany felt that she'd had quite enough of their attention and couldn't stand it a minute more. She shooed them out of the bedroom, and they left without further protest, satisfied that their prince would be pleased with his new mistress.

That thought clung and grew disturbing tentacles in Bethany's mind as she stared at the bed. Was Zakr married? Did Arab sheikhs practise monogamy, or did they have many wives and mistresses? All she knew was the undoubtable fact that he was a very knowing lover, which surely meant a lot of experience with women.

How many times had a woman been prepared for him in this way? Was it usual or unusual? She should have thought to question her attendants. Her ability to think on her feet seemed to be slipping away from her.

On the other hand, Prince Zakr's power made the question irrelevant, anyway. The end was inevitable and it was probably better that she didn't know about his other women. She could pretend . . . Bethany shook her head, not wanting to examine the complex emotions that were being aroused by the man who would take her tonight.

She walked over to one of the windows and looked out, trying to concentrate her mind on something else. Escape. That was what she should be thinking of. But there was no balcony, and the ground was three storeys below her. Her eye was caught by the scaffolding near the end of the building, some thirty metres away. Apparently some repairs were being made to the roof. The pipe structure triggered an idea.

Bethany's routine on the uneven bars had always brought her very good scores in her years of competition in gymnastics. If she could get to that scaffolding, she was certain she could swing her way safely down to the ground. But then . . . how to get past the high wall that surrounded the place? And she really needed a jeep once she was out in the desert.

'Only a bird could escape from here, Bethany.'

Her heart leapt as though she had been physically caught by surprise, yet it was only his soft voice winding around her, turning her towards him. He was on the other side of the room, near the door which she hadn't heard open or close, and the sight of him caught the breath in her throat.

He was dressed in pure white, except for the gold sash around his waist and the gold and black twisted *'iqal* that held the head-dress in place. The neckline of his tunic was much the same as hers—high and round—but slashed to the breastline, its edge embroidered in gold thread. The trousers beneath the tunic were baggy but caught in at the ankles, giving him an exotic look that was none the less extremely masculine. The thin, thong-like sandals on his feet were black.

Bethany was completely tongue-tied. It was crazy! He was so foreign, terribly different from any man she had ever had anything to do with, yet he attracted her with such irresistible force that her mind could not dredge up any effective defence against her body's response to him.

Her sharp swing away from the window had stopped him in his step. He stared at her as she stared at him, drinking in every detail of her appearance. Their frozen stillness and the silent tension which bound them to each other seemed to magnify the long expulsion of his breath before he spoke.

'This is how a woman should look ... to make her lover forget the cares of the day and look forward to the pleasures of the night.'

The words shook Bethany into a sudden panic. It was one thing to accept an inevitability in theory, but the actuality was upon her now, and, however compellingly attractive he was to her, it was wrong to give in to him. Such a spineless surrender negated all the principles she had worked by and lived for throughout her life.

'Zakr...' She almost swallowed the name she had forced off her tongue. He had resumed his walk across the room to her, and each pace he took weakened her resolve. She wanted him to reach her...touch her...take her in his arms and make her forget everything else.

It was wicked...wanton...stupid, stupid, stupid, her mind screamed in a last desperate bid for sanity. 'Zakr, please, don't do this...' The words choked through her trembling lips. She lifted her hand in a fluttering bid to fend him off.

He caught it, lifted it slowly to his mouth, and pressed a warm kiss into her palm. His dark eyes softly probed the painful confusion in hers as he lowered her hand, his strong fingers stroking across the erratic pulse in her wrist as he spoke.

'A caged bird comes to accept the pleasant security of its confinement, and does not leave, even when the door is open. So it will be with you, Bethany. You will come to accept...'

'No! I must go!' she cried in agonised denial. 'Please, reconsider what you are doing, Zakr. You must know it can only hurt me. Please...there can't be any real need for you to...'

His finger moved over her lips, effectively silencing her, and in that same instant Bethany realised that her plea had effected the opposite reaction to its purpose.

His expression hardened, and the glimmer of sympathetic understanding was gone. It seemed to conflict with everything she knew about him, but pain looked back at her, evidenced in the tightened line of his mouth, the slight contortion of the muscles in his face, the sharpened blackness of his eyes.

'There is every need. Do not ask of me what I cannot give, Bethany. It has gone past the time when I might have chosen differently.'

He pulled her into a fiercely possessive embrace, his arms encircling her, crushing her against him. His mouth swept across her hair with devouring ownership, and Bethany's head swam with the intense passion of the moment. Then, even as she began to think that he did care for her, that she meant more to him than a night's pleasure, he spoke and confused her even further.

'Your body is so slight and soft, yet there is a strength in you that calls to me. But however urgently I feel my need, I shall not hurt you.'

He withdrew the support of his arms to cup her face, and Bethany clutched convulsively at his tunic, fearful of falling. Her legs did not seem to belong to her any more, and her body was shot through with aching weakness. As she looked up into the dark vortex of his eyes she felt she was drowning in a relentless sea of emotion that washed away any chance of self-survival.

'You have nothing to fear from me, I promise you. There is a right time for every fruit to be plucked, and this is your time. You showed me your readiness this afternoon. Let it be . . . as it should be. All is prepared. Come with me . . . be with me . . . join with me.'

The soft, seductive words drained any last thought of resistance. He drew her arm around his waist and held her close to him, his arm curved possessively around her shoulders as he took her out of the bedroom.

Bethany accompanied him like a sleepwalker, helpless to do anything but move at his command. When they entered another room, she was too dazed by what was happening to appreciate its opulence. Her eyes only received impressions that floated in meaningless patterns around her.

Music was being played—soft, haunting tunes. It came from the end of the room where a small stage had been curtained off. A shower of threaded gold beads fell in front of it, casting artistic shadows that obscured the faint outline of the musicians.

The room was softly lit by brass filigree lanterns, hung by chains from a ceiling of gold lattice. Rich rugs and cushions were strewn about the floor. Chaise-longues upholstered in gleaming, brocaded velvet were arranged around low tables with ornate gold legs and marble surfaces.

An exotic gold cupola hung from the ceiling over the centre of the room, and underneath it was set a very low round table which was absolutely laden with a feast of delicacies. A curved and many-cushioned lounge-seat extended around the table, and Zakr lifted Bethany off her feet and laid her on this, propping the upper half of her body up with cushions.

He tossed more cushions on to the floor beside her and sank down on to them, sitting adjacent to her so that his face was close to hers and his arm rested lightly on her waist. 'You have nothing to say, Bethany?' he asked, his voice teasing, his dark eyes raking her out of passivity.

'Would it change anything?' she asked, recognising the futility of fighting his will.

'No.'

The flat negative somehow eased the burden of responsibility from Bethany's heart. Her conscience was appeased.

He clapped his hands in sharp signal for something to happen. Bethany was aware of the opening and closing of a door, but she could not tear her gaze from the teasing gleam in those darkly knowing eyes. Did he know that he had just released her from the need to keep fighting him? Did he know that she wanted him to love her...just a little?

She was trembling even before he touched her, and all he did was stroke the back of a finger up her throat to tilt her chin higher, so that her face was turned to his.

'I promised I would ravish all your senses. And with this I begin,' he murmured. His hand lifted past her and his gaze flicked up in sharp command. 'The perfume of the Pharaohs.'

The startled gasp drew Bethany's attention to the attendant who had carried in a wooden tray loaded with little bottles and jars. He was old and he spoke in a tremulous but chiding voice.

'Sire, that can only be used by those of royal blood.'

'Just so,' Zakr affirmed quietly, not taking offence at the old man's respect for tradition. 'And I shall use it . . . where I will.'

'Your will is my will,' came the chastened reply. The tiniest bottle on the tray was placed in Zakr's hand.

'Go now.'

The old man left the room without another word.

Bethany suddenly recalled Zakr's questioning her about the McGregor motto. Of royal blood . . . had he interpreted her words literally this afternoon? Feeling quite agitated about being given an honour that was not her due, Bethany felt she ought to protest; but Zakr had already unstoppered the tiny bottle and poured some of the precious liquid on to his finger.

'It takes over ten man-years to make a bottle of this size,' he informed her as he started dabbing the perfume behind her ears. The scent was so exquisitely tantalising that Bethany's protest died without utterance. A drift of sandalwood, combined with the mystery of the East . . . attar and frangipani with musk and violets and jasmine . . . it was beyond definition as the oil reacted with her skin, leaving behind layer after layer of tantalising aroma.

With the slow deliberation of one performing a ceremony, he anointed her temples with the oily essence; and the aroma built, taking on even more subtle nuances. He smoothed it into the hollow of her throat, then parted the neckline of her gown and drew it down to the valley between her breasts.

His hand slid under the embroidered fabric and spread over her wildly beating heart. Bethany looked up at him, half intoxicated by the perfume, and drowning in the knowledge that her heart was his, to do with as he willed.

'No other perfume in the world equals this,' he told her in a low, intimate murmur. 'The secret of its making was brought from Egypt during the *Hijrah* in 642. The high priest of Luxor was beheaded so that the formula could never be revealed to anyone else. It has remained ours, and ours alone, ever since that time. You are now wearing what was once worn by Cleopatra.'

Bethany's heart beat faster. The honour he was doing her was far beyond anything she had expected from him. She barely gave cognisance to the cold brutality dealt to the Egyptian priest by Zakr's ancestors. The perfume was fit for a queen, and he had bestowed it on her. 'Thank you,' she whispered.

His hand trailed up and curled around her neck. He smiled down at her. 'It is your first time,' he said. 'Every proper step must be taken so that you will have memories of this night which will reach over all your life.'

His fingers raked through her hair, and his hand dropped away to replace the stopper in the tiny bottle of perfume and carefully set it on the table.

Without his touch to distract her, Bethany's mind fully grasped what he had just said. The simplicity of his intent jarred her out of her entranced daze. It was all so coldly calculated to impress. There was no love here, no rampant desire that could not be controlled. This was just a process he put women through. She had been fooling herself, wanting to believe she was someone really special to him.

The tension in her stomach rippled with cramp. The blackest of jealousies ripped through her heart. 'How many first times have there been for you?' she cried. 'How many wives...women...have you tied to you like this? Why pick on me? Why?'

His eyes seared her into silence. 'Because you will give me what I want, Bethany,' he said with an intensity that shook her.

She shrank back against the cushions, her hand lifting to ward him off. 'No, I won't!' she choked, her sense of pride tearing into weak shreds under the power of his dark attraction.

He followed her down on to the cushions, his body half covering hers. For one fierce moment his eyes blazed their intent, then his mouth was on hers, drawing the passion of mad jealousy into the more feverish passion of desire. And her traitorous hands slid up over the strongly muscled shoulders and around his neck, instinctively possessive, just as her body pressed closer, blindly seeking his possession.

He withdrew the erotic plunder of his mouth, but his lips did not separate from her own. They rubbed lightly over the sensitised tissues, and for Bethany this gentle touching was exquisite torture.

'You will give me what I want?' he whispered, still sustaining the tormenting contact.

'Yes,' she moaned, barely knowing what she was saying, only that she wanted him.

But he did not satisfy her craving. He pulled back, and when Bethany lifted her lashes to meet his eyes in urgent appeal his dark gaze was still burning with purpose.

'There have been women for me, Bethany, but none I keep. I was married until two years ago. My wife was what you would call an arranged bride, but I was fond of her. She bore me two daughters before she died in an accident that should never have happened.'

A grim savagery hardened his expression for a moment, and Bethany shivered at the thought of what punishment had been meted out to those responsible for the accident which had caused his wife's death.

'But you, Bethany...' A note of deep satisfaction throbbed into his voice. 'You are of a different mettle. You will bear me a son. And I will have a son. I must have a son.'

His hands stroked down over her peaking breasts, and caressed the slight mound of her stomach with a kind of hungry reverence for the womb that would carry his seed. 'It shall be so,' he murmured, and bent to press his cheek against the shocked heave of her flesh.

His voice wafted slowly to her dazed ears. 'We will make a son who can hold together the changing forces of our world and wield them to his will. It must be done. It will be done.'

CHAPTER SEVEN

His son... the shock-waves kept rolling through Bethany's mind... Zakr wanted her to bear his son! She had wanted proof that he did not regard her lightly, but this...this was the most serious, far-reaching claim he could possibly make on her; and she was horrified by the cold-blooded calculation behind his seduction.

'You don't care what I feel. Or what happens to me,' she said in a harshly driven voice that was barely recognisable as her own.

She heard him sigh, and when he lifted his head his eyes met the turbulent accusation in hers with a haunting need. 'On the contrary. I will take the greatest possible care of you.'

Only because she would be carrying his child, Bethany thought fiercely. Then was totally riven by the thought that it would be her child, too. The sudden tug at her heart confused and dissipated the outrage that sanity insisted she should keep feeling. To have a child...his son...her baby. The idea tunnelled into her subconscious, finding a deep-seated need for the fulfilment that a baby would give her.

'Bethany...'

His hand cupped her cheek, his thumb tracing the line of her lower lip with the same tantalising sureness that had enthralled her this morning in his tent, and Bethany felt totally mesmerised by the dark intensity of his eyes. They seemed to draw on her soul, impressing his mastery of her innermost being.

'You will feel the power of my love, Bethany.' His hand slid slowly down her throat, and once again sought to rest over her palpitating heart. 'And you will be satisfied in a way you never thought possible.'

Her mind argued that he was exulting over her vulnerability to him, which he was exploiting so skilfully; yet she was helpless even to stop her own hand reaching out to spread over his heart in an instinctive bid to claim him as he was claiming her. He caught it, raised it to his throat and slid it down inside the neckline of his tunic.

The electric contact with his bare chest curled her fingers into a fist, and his eyes flashed with satisfaction at her dry little gasp. 'We shall drink to the fruit of our union,' he said, as if the whole matter was settled beyond all question.

Bethany shuddered as he released her. The sense of loss was deep and immediate and faintly chilling. He could touch her or not touch her at will, without there being any discernible effect on him either way, while she was left with every nerve-end humming like the taut strings of a harp that could only be brought to vibrant life by the touch of its master.

He turned back to her, having poured liquid into a silver goblet. 'Drink with me,' he commanded softly, curling her hand around his as he lifted the rim of the goblet to her lips.

Even though she still mentally recoiled from having motherhood thrust upon her in such an arbitrary way, Bethany did as she was bid, too emotionally confused to disobey him.

Just as the perfume had teased her sense of smell, so did the drink tease her taste-buds, proving impossible to define...sweet, but with a dry after-taste, full of fruity tang, yet so subtly blended that no specific flavour sprang to mind.

'And now let me tempt your appetite.'

The round table-top was apparently connected to a mechanism which allowed Zakr to spin it around. He did so slowly, enumerating the many delicacies which had been set out on silver trays.

'...pickled quail's eggs; slivers of smoked salmon; the pink wonder of coral trout; succulent oysters; the delicate flesh of the *dugong*; fruit ripened in the tropics; a range of the best and tastiest foods from all around the world. Just to tempt you. Tell me what you would like and I will serve you.'

Bethany shook her head. Food was the last thing she wanted in her churning stomach.

'It is a long time since you've eaten,' he reminded her. The tantalising half-smile curled his mouth. 'If you faint, I do not want it to be from hunger, Bethany.'

He selected a small portion of crabmeat covered with caviar and egg-yolk, and lifted it to her mouth. 'Try this,' he commanded.

Clearly there was no refusing him, and Bethany dutifully ate. He plied her with more food, and after the first few mouthfuls she began to enjoy the tasty morsels he kept insisting she try. Even her stomach was soothed.

She *was* hungry. She had eaten nothing since the sweet biscuits in his tent this morning. She was probably light-headed from hunger, which might account for her muddled thinking and the physical weakness. Besides, while Zakr was feeding her he was not touching her. Not in any way which induced that slavish mindlessness in her.

For the first time since Zakr had entered the bedroom, Bethany could think clearly, and her brain moved into high-drive. She could not deny the strong appeal of having his child, but she had to argue against it. The leap into the unknown was far too great. She could not accept it.

'What if I don't conceive? What will you do with me then?' she asked as levelly as she could.

His eyes actually sparkled. 'I do not think I will tire of you, Bethany. In fact, I may very well find it difficult to keep away from you, even to perform the administrative duties that are required of me during the day. My nights will most assuredly be yours. You will conceive, sooner or later.'

'What if I can't?' she persisted, even though her body betrayed her, heating and squirming inside at the thought of being held by Zakr night after night.

He flicked her a sceptical look. 'If you were barren, you would have told me before this, Bethany.' Again that half-smile. 'I have a healthy respect for the ingenuity of your mind. It is one of the reasons why I have chosen you to be the mother of my son.'

'And what if I have a daughter, instead?' she taunted angered by the unemotional deliberation behind his choice.

Relentless purpose answered her. 'Then we try again. And again. Until you do give birth to the son I must have. You are young and strong, Bethany, and I will keep you safe.'

Keep her imprisoned, he meant. Bethany did not doubt she would be installed with every possible luxury—she was having a taste of it right now, and she couldn't deny its appeal, either—but it was still a prison.

And her father was probably rotting in some other prison, without anything or anyone to comfort him. She had to escape!

'Some melon? Strawberries?'

He smiled his pleasure in her eager acceptance of what he was offering, and Bethany's heart lurched. It hurt, the thought of leaving him, never seeing him again.

The urge to please him, to give him the son he wanted of her, almost overwhelmed her resolve. But he was a tyrant, her mind argued; a tyrant who would stop at nothing to get his own way. How could she even begin to love such a person? What she felt for him was sexual attraction. Nothing more!

She had to get away before he drained all her will-power and swallowed up her life. 'Have my things from the jeep been recovered?' she asked, trying to keep their importance to her out of her voice.

He nodded. 'And your suitcase from P.J. Weatherly's apartment. He was most relieved to hear you were in my safe custody.'

His grin held an almost boyish mischief, and was so infectious that Bethany found herself grinning back at him. Poor P.J. Weatherly! She had undoubtedly given him one headache after another.

But it did not help her that P.J. believed she was safe! It was going to be very difficult explaining the situation if she ever got free; and that thought wiped the smile off her face. 'I want those things returned to me, Zakr,' she said with more force than she had intended.

He raised a questioning eyebrow, and the twinkle faded from his eyes. 'Why? You have no need of them here.'

Bethany frantically cast through her mind for an acceptable argument. 'Your women servants wouldn't supply me with underclothes.'

He threw back his head and laughed, a happy, joyous sound that played havoc with her pulse even before his hand brushed over her breast, fanning her nipple into excited prominence.

'Is it not exciting to know that you are more accessible to my touch? Does it not make you more aware of being a woman, Bethany?' he teased wickedly.

'I am not going to walk around all day without underclothes!' she retorted, desperately fighting the ripples of sensation coursing through her body.

He laughed again and lifted his hand to her flushed face to stroke the heated colour in her cheeks. 'You may have your clothes, but remember that I do not want to see you in them.'

'And if you want to keep me healthy I must have my medical supplies, too,' she insisted. 'There are tablets I must take as a precaution against malaria.'

A glint of suspicion sharpened his eyes. 'You have a lot of medical supplies, Bethany.'

'That's because I'm a nurse,' she explained quickly. 'A nurse is trained to be ready for any emergency.'

His hand slid up to the pulse at her temple. 'A precaution against pregnancy?'

'No! I . . . I never thought of it.' Fool that she was! But how could she have ever imagined this situation?

He nodded, satisfied. 'They will be brought to you tomorrow.'

'Thank you,' she sighed in relief.

'After I have them checked through,' he added pointedly, letting her know that he was leaving nothing on trust where she was concerned.

'Fine,' she agreed without hesitation.

And he relaxed, smiling once more. 'I think it is time that we finished this meal.'

Every nerve-end in Bethany's body leapt with treacherous anticipation, and she knew that he saw naked vulnerability in her eyes, because his gleamed with triumphant satisfaction. It shamed her that she could not control her physical reaction to him, particularly as she saw no complementary reaction from him.

He clapped his hands sharply and servants came pouring into the room to remove the trays of food.

Coffee was ordered and brought, along with dishes of Turkish Delight, tiny balls of coconut ice, and paper-thin wafers of white and dark chocolate.

It was all too evident that Zakr was intent on pleasuring her in every way, but he was also retaining a control that Bethany vowed she would break before this night was over. The desire for some power over him was so strong that she came very close to losing all perspective on their relationship.

He would take her tonight. That was inescapable. And she wanted it to happen. There was no point in fooling herself that she didn't. But any relationship between them could only be a sexual one. That was all he wanted...a means to an end. To become emotionally involved with Zakr Tahnun Sadiq was only courting disaster for herself. And her father.

What she had to keep remembering were the days in between the nights; the times when she would be free of his presence. Only then would she have any chance of getting away.

She drank the ritual three cups of coffee and ate a few of the sweets he offered her. Then he made a slow, sensual exercise of wiping her mouth and hands with one of the moist towels that had been provided in a warming-bowl.

He cleansed each of her fingers separately with a teasing gentleness that made Bethany feel like screaming. And all the time his eyes burned into hers, wickedly aware of the build-up of tension that she was desperately trying to control.

'I think I hate you, Zakr,' she said on a bursting wave of pent-up feeling.

'No. That is not what you feel, Bethany. It is the waiting that has become unbearable. All your other senses are now sated. Except one. And that is better not hurried.'

'I want you to get it over with,' she muttered, tears of frustration and resentment welling into her eyes. Didn't he want her as much as she wanted him? Didn't he feel any need for her, apart from the purpose she was expected to serve?

'I do not want to hurt you, Bethany,' he said, and the sudden tone of tenderness confused her emotions further, particularly when he followed the words with a sweetly gentle kiss that soothed the fretting edges of her nerves.

'I am glad you did not let the women prepare you,' he murmured, pressing warm little kisses all over her face. 'You do me an honour that I will always treasure. Do not ask me to abuse it.'

'What honour?' Bethany asked in bewilderment.

His eyes smiled into hers. 'It is the custom in this country that the women attend to the maidenhood of a virgin so that there will be no discomfort for her. That you insisted on remaining inviolate for me is the bestowal of a great gift.'

'Oh!' Bethany's eyes widened in shocked understanding. She hadn't realised what he had meant this afternoon when she had argued over the bathing arrangements. Thank God she had kept those women away from her!

'It pleases me very much that you didn't want anyone's touch but mine,' Zakr continued, sliding his arms under her knees and shoulders.

He lifted her in one seemingly effortless heave, while Bethany's mind was still whirling with what he had told her. It was barbaric! Or was it more practically civilised than her own society? It was difficult to know anything for certain any more.

She couldn't even remember linking her hands behind Zakr's neck, but they were there, clinging tightly to him as he carried her out of the room. His arms held her cradled against his chest, and she gave in to the temptation to snuggle her head on to his broad shoulder. The sigh that whispered from her lips was one of pleasurable surrender. There was something very reassuring about a powerful man.

The bedroom was lit by a single lamp. Its gold silk shade was edged by beaded tassels that threw soft shadows over the furnishings. Zakr stood Bethany on her feet, and kissed her long and deeply while he dislodged her grasp around his neck and lowered her hands to her sides. Then his own hands lifted briefly to her face before sliding down her throat and spreading the neckline of her caftan wide to push it over her shoulders.

Zakr left Bethany's mouth tingling with erotic sensation when he stepped back a pace. Her eyes fixed on him in glazed appeal, but his gaze was avidly fastened on the white smoothness of her shoulders. Very slowly, he pushed her gown down her arms.

She felt the pressure of the embroidered fabric sliding down the firm swell of her breasts, pausing near their peak. His fingers brushed softly over her bared flesh, then slowly eased the tightly stretched silk past her nipples, releasing them from all confinement.

A guttural exclamation broke from Zakr's lips. 'Never have I seen such breasts on a woman,' he whispered huskily. 'Never such perfection. You are...exquisitely beautiful!'

Muscle-tone from all her gymnast years, Bethany thought dizzily. It was the last coherent thought she had. Her mind exploded with sensation when Zakr bent to kiss each nipple in turn. She struggled to lift her hands to him, but they were still caught in the long sleeves of her gown.

'Zakr...please...' she begged helplessly, not quite knowing what she was begging for, only that her body was once more out of control.

His long, supple fingers stroked the silk down her body, over her stomach, her hips, her thighs, until the gown fell uselessly at her feet. And again he stepped back from her, his gaze burning over all that had been revealed. Bethany's skin heated and chilled in turn under his total absorption in her body. He reached out and touched the apricot-gold hair between her thighs, his fingers threading the tight curls.

'Zakr...' The choked gasp protested against the weakness that his caress was inducing in her legs.

He caught her as she swayed towards him, and lifted her on to the bed, laying her down with a slow deliberation that sprayed her hair out over the pillows. He stroked the fanned-out tresses for several moments before trailing his fingers back down to her thighs.

'You are...unbelievably magnificent,' he said huskily. 'More than any man should have...'

A primitive little thrill of exultation ran through Bethany's heart. She did have some power over Zakr, enough to fur his voice with desire. And there was an urgent haste in his movements as he discarded his clothes. She was absolutely certain he was no longer thinking of the son he wanted.

He was not playing with her now.

He was in deadly earnest.

He wanted her.

Bethany didn't even think of moving or trying to cover herself up. She exulted that Zakr couldn't tear his eyes off her, and she was totally fascinated by what was being revealed of him.

His hair was pitch-black, cropped short and shaped around neat, close-set ears. It gave his face a sleekly handsome look. His body was tautly muscled and beautifully proportioned, and his skin gleamed richly in the dim lamplight.

The all too evident potency of his manhood sent a funny little quiver through Bethany's stomach; a quiver that spread swiftly to her legs when he stepped forward and caressed the sensitive inner sides of her thighs, gently persuading them apart.

He knelt over her, one knee between hers, and for one frightening moment he again looked like a bird of prey about to swoop; but he lowered his long, lean body to one side of her and pulled her close to him, making their first full naked contact a movingly gentle one.

Bethany trembled violently, her skin reacting with almost electric shock to the touch of his. His mouth moved sensually over hers, not seeking to invade, and his hand stroked her back with a tantalising lightness that made her shudder with pleasure.

Her hand moved to touch him, dragging experimentally up the lean flesh of his hip. She felt the slight contraction underneath her fingertips, and in the same instant he shuddered uncontrollably, his chest rising and falling in violent reaction. The thrill of her power to excite him made Bethany bolder.

She stroked the vibrant tautness of his manhood, and Zakr went completely out of control, slamming her body against his, rolling her on to her back, crushing her underneath him as his mouth exploded into hers with an erotic force that fired Bethany into wild response.

Her hands clawed up his back and clutched his head, but he tore free of her hold, covering her throat and shoulders with feverish kisses that left her skin flushed with tingling heat. She tried to catch him back, but he slid out of her grasp, devouring her breasts with a fierce hunger that drove piercing shafts of exquisite sensation through her entire body.

She cried out; she moaned; her fingers raked and tugged his hair in mindless ecstasy; and Zakr was merciless in his erotic plunder, his tongue thrashing her nipples, his mouth drawing on her throbbing flesh as if he could never have enough of it.

'Please ... please ... now!' she begged, her body instinctively arching its offer, her hands dragging at his shoulders in urgent need for him.

Gentle fingers parted her tender flesh, softly stroking her towards chaotic madness. Her fingernails dug into her palms. Her whole body clenched with a tension so great that she felt every cell was about to explode.

'Zakr ... you've got to stop,' she screamed. 'Please ... I can't ... I can't ...'

Her voice trailed into a sob of need, and he moved swiftly to take her into the final realm of intimacy. His hand slid under her hips, lifting them higher, and she wanted that first thrust of him inside her so much that she moaned in grateful relief when it came.

It was the most exquisite sensation in the world to feel that strong, heavy fullness inside her. Unbelievably satisfying. When he started to withdraw she cried out in protest, flinging her arms around him and urging him back.

He came, again and again, in a fierce, stroking rhythm that awakened the savage in her. Her hips surged against his. Her nails raked down his back and dug into his buttocks. She bit his shoulder. And the harsh rasp of his breath was wild music to her ears.

Her passion for him was so intense that the first ecstatic melting of her body brought only a brief limpness to her limbs. Her mind had closed down long ago, and every sense begged for that sweet, aching pleasure to suffuse through her again and again. She ran her hands down Zakr's heaving chest, and deliberately sought those erotic areas under his stomach.

It drove him wild, and she spilled from climax to climax, glorying in the explosive tension of his body until he too expelled the long, shuddering sigh of release. Then she wrapped her legs around him, holding him inside her even when he collapsed forward. He hugged her just as tightly to him, rolling on to his side when she struggled for breath from his crushing weight.

His mouth swept across the silky strands of her fringe, planting fervent little kisses on her brow. 'The embers of your fire will burn in me for ever,' he murmured. 'There cannot be another like you, Bethany.'

'Nor you,' she whispered back, and snuggled her head contentedly under his chin.

His hand played possessively over the curve of her back. 'Then you will never leave me?'

A pain of terrible uncertainty twisted through Bethany's heart. 'Not now,' she answered truthfully. Not this minute. Not this night. She never wanted this wonderful intimacy to end. How could she leave him when he could make her feel like this?

Her mind shied away from the enormity of such a loss, and yet her conscience dictated that she would soon have to consider it. The memory of her father could not be blotted out ... not for ever.

'Hold me, Zakr! Keep holding me,' she cried, suddenly feeling a desperate need for the security of his arms around her.

'I won't ever let you go, Bethany,' he assured her, and pressed her closer.

She relaxed against him, content just to be held and soothed. She did not think about whether a baby had been conceived. Zakr cradled her in the crook of his arm, her face against his chest, and she listened contentedly to his strong heartbeat. It called to her, promising a life she had never known before...a blissful fulfilment...peace. And Bethany closed her eyes to everything else and slept.

CHAPTER EIGHT

THE FIRST wave of consciousness came and Bethany resisted it. She didn't have the strength to wrench her eyes open, and it was much, much easier to slide back to sleep. Except she was missing something. Something that she wanted . . . needed. Her brow puckered over the problem, and her arm swept slowly across the bed in a blind search for what should have been there to make her feel right again. She heaved a little sigh of discouragement when nothing answered her need.

'It is past midday.'

The voice was soft and indulgent, and there was a warm smile in the words that curved her own mouth with sensual pleasure. Zakr. He had not left her.

The memory of last night's mind-shattering passion rippled through her sluggish mind, startling Bethany into rolling over and opening her eyes. Zakr was seated at the end of the bed, fully dressed, and wearing an expression of deep satisfaction.

'You are beautiful to watch when you are asleep.'

'How long have you been watching me?' Bethany half yawned, stretching in a languorous way that was unconsciously provocative.

He smiled and stood up to move closer to her, picking up her outflung hand as he sat down again. 'Long enough to see you reach out for me,' he said, planting a warm kiss on to her palm before leaning over and pressing a more lingering kiss on her mouth.

Bethany's arms curled around his neck, and a sigh of happy contentment whispered from her lips as he remained leaning over her, his darkly handsome face close to hers. She vaguely wondered why she had ever thought him austere-looking. And his eyes weren't the least bit hard or commanding. They were black velvet.

'Did I hurt you last night?' he asked, and the caring note in his voice warmed her heart.

'I haven't had time to notice,' she replied with ingenuous truth.

He laughed and teasingly stroked her cheek. 'I think perhaps you deliberately drove me to excesses that I hadn't planned at all. But I am not sorry if it pleased you.'

A triumphant grin lit her face at the memory of his wild loss of control. 'Perhaps you deserved a bit of your own treatment back.'

'Treatment?' he queried with an amused lift of his eyebrow.

'You can't expect to have everything your own way with me,' she told him archly.

'No?' he mocked, and kissed her with more intense purpose.

'No,' Bethany breathed when her wits had settled back into order again.

He laughed as though her answer delighted him. 'Well, my little enchantress, what would you like to do this afternoon? I am at your disposal,' he said grandly, but there was a wickedly suggestive glint in his eyes.

As severely tempted as she was to experience his lovemaking again, Bethany decided that she did not want him to become sated with her. Hadn't her father always told her that anything that was too easy was very quickly taken for granted?

And there was the problem of her father. She still had to do something about finding him, no matter how much she wanted to stay with Zakr.

'Bethany...'

His fingertips brushed her chin and her eyes flew up to meet a sharply probing gaze.

'What is wrong?'

'I was thinking of my father,' she answered bluntly.

He frowned. 'There is nothing you can do about him. You are with me now. You are not to be concerned about your father any more.'

It was a command. A dismissal of her father that Bethany couldn't stomach, but she swallowed her bitter disappointment, all too aware that intransigence would not get her anywhere. Any power she had over Zakr was far too new to flex against his will when he had so obviously made up his mind that her father was dead. However, she could not quite hold her tongue. If Zakr really cared for her...

'I came to this country to find my father, Zakr,' she reminded him quietly.

'But you will stay for me!' His eyes flashed with black jealousy as he pulled away from her and stood up, once more a steely figure of authority. 'Let me hear no more talk of your father. That matter is finished as far as you are concerned.'

He clapped his hands and servants came rushing in. He gave orders for Bethany to be bathed and dressed and delivered to him in time for lunch. Then he turned back to Bethany.

'I have had your possessions brought here as you wished. You will respect my wishes as I have yours. Is that clear, Bethany?'

'Yes,' she replied in a very small voice, deeply hurt by the loss of empathy with him.

He stalked out of the room without another word, leaving Bethany feeling very much at odds with herself. And with him.

In the clear light of day, she didn't like being dictated to. She might be his prisoner, but Zakr needn't start thinking she was his slave. She had a good mind to pull the bedcovers over her head and go back to sleep. She felt so dreadfully tired that closing her eyes again seemed like an exceptionally good idea.

However, she didn't suppose mutiny at this point would be in her best interests, and the women Zakr had called in were not about to leave her alone. One of them held out a gorgeous dressing-gown for her to slip on, and Bethany decided she might as well co-operate. After all, if she was ever to escape, she did need to see more of this hunting lodge than the bedroom!

The bath did not take away the lethargy that seemed to drag at her limbs. Was it jet-lag, Bethany wondered, or the concentrated activity of the last few days, or the aftermath of those extraordinary sensations through her body last night? Whatever the cause, she felt totally drained of energy.

When she was ushered into Zakr's presence, his keen gaze instantly picked up her listlessness. He dismissed the servants, and in a complete reversal of manner from his previous leave-taking, he drew Bethany into a gentle embrace and stroked her hair away from her face in soft concern.

'You feel sore and tender?'

'No. Just deadly tired,' she replied, although Zakr's embrace was having the effect of pumping more life through her veins.

He frowned. 'You have taken on too much for a woman. I admire you for it, but it is not the way nature ordained it. A woman should have a man to protect her and deal with everything.'

And so much for equality of the sexes, Bethany thought, but she did not really dislike Zakr's view of the natural order of things.

Nevertheless, she did have a mind of her own, and she could never be at one with a man who refused to discuss the decisions he made, most particularly those which related to her personally.

Then Zakr smiled down at her, and Bethany's mental independence felt very shaky.

'You will feel better tomorrow if you force yourself to exercise this afternoon. We will walk around the grounds after we have eaten lunch,' he proclaimed. His smile spread into a grin of happy anticipation. 'Then tonight we will make love, and you will sleep deeply and well.'

With Zakr in her company all the time, there was no possibility of running away, Bethany thought, and she did not even notice that the thought caused her no dismay. In fact, if she had examined her feelings with any serious attempt at self-perception, she would have found a deep relief that was cushioned on an even deeper sense of sheer joy.

All throughout lunch Zakr questioned Bethany about her nursing experience, and she told him of her training, her work in the casualty wards during emergencies, and her more recent theatre-duties, assisting Dr Hong in the serious surgery he performed with such deft skill.

'You can bear to watch such things?' he asked curiously.

'The workings of our bodies are fascinating and wonderful, Zakr. And I desperately want each patient to be made well again,' she explained. 'We're doing a job that has to be done. That's how I think of it.'

He nodded, his eyes glowing approval at her. 'I will have a new hospital built. The best equipment money can buy, and the most highly skilled medical staff. People who can train my people. It is a problem getting them here.'

Bethany instantly thought of Matron Vaughan, but without having first checked the working conditions in the other hospitals she could not, in faith, put forward the Matron's name. 'I would like to see one of your hospitals some time, Zakr,' she said eagerly.

He frowned and shook his head. 'You would not be pleased. Too many sick people. And there is a risk of your picking up some harmful infection. You cannot go.'

'But that's ridiculous!' Bethany protested. 'I've worked with sick people for years and...'

'Bethany, you are always arguing with me,' he interrupted curtly. 'I will not take any chances with your well-being. That is my will. There is nothing more to be said,' he added, the black eyes flashing home the emphasis.

Bethany stifled a sigh, recalling the old perfume servant's reply to Zakr last night: 'Your will is my will.' If he had been hearing that sort of nonsense all his life he was not going to appreciate her bucking the system. And after all, it was rather nice that he felt so protective of her. Or was that only because he wanted her to be the mother of his son?

Her feelings about Zakr were getting more and more confused, and it didn't help when he reached over and took her hand. His smile demolished every bit of common sense she had.

'Come! I shall take you for a walk. We will talk of more pleasant things,' he said indulgently.

Bethany smiled back and rose from the table with him, happy to do his bidding on this occasion. Lunch had been a very pleasant meal—a spicy chicken dish and a delicious fruit salad, followed by the inevitable cups of coffee—the conversation had not provoked any difficult tension between them. Besides, the possessive way he looked at her and fondled her hand made Bethany feel beautiful.

There was very little in the way of gardens or lawns around the hunting lodge. Palm-trees provided most of the greenery. Bethany surmised that the heat of the desert kept most people indoors, anyway. The attendants they met on their walk were invariably ensconced in shady places.

Zakr led Bethany to the stables where the thoroughbred white Arabian horses were kept. He knew them all by name, and many of them whinnied a return greeting. They were certainly magnificent animals and Zakr proudly showed them off, giving long pedigrees to some of them.

Next he showed her the kennels for his saluki hounds. The dogs bounded out to his whistle, and Bethany admired their lean grace and strength. They seemed terribly elegant to be hunting dogs, but Zakr insisted they were the best and she could not disbelieve him. Zakr would not be content with anything less than the best.

Which surely made her the best woman in his eyes, Bethany thought with immense satisfaction. At least for the time being, her mind tagged on as a caution to runaway elation. But he was a prince, and he could have chosen almost anyone, she argued smugly.

'How do you spend your time?' she asked, curious to know more about him.

'Usually I hunt three days a week. It is not obligatory, but for over five thousand years it has been our tradition.' He sliced her a teasing smile. 'If something more important needs attention...then of course it takes precedence.'

More important! Was she more important to him than his tradition? 'Was this one of your hunting days?' she couldn't resist asking.

He shrugged. 'I sent out a scouting party. It is best that we know where to hunt before setting out.'

Bethany felt disappointed until she caught his eyes laughing at her. He had known she was fishing for the compliment, and was deliberately teasing her. He *had* given up his hunting to be with her, she was sure of it. A happy triumph soared through her heart. Bethany was suddenly so enamoured with the man at her side that she barely noticed where he steered her until they were inside the mews which housed all the falcons.

The birds were kept in very superior quarters. Their homes were clean and airy, and Bethany found herself musing whether the people themselves had better housing. Clearly Zakr prized his collection of birds even above his horses and hounds, and he took immense pleasure in illustrating the differences between the goshawks, the peregrine falcons, and all the other varieties.

Last of all, and in pride of place, was the great Greenland gyrfalcon that had been the cause of Bethany's fateful meeting with Zakr at Rhafhar airport.

The huge white bird was attached to a perch by two straps of fine silk which ended in a ring. Over her head she wore a hood. Zakr's hand reached out and gently caressed her plumage, and the strong glint of possession in his eyes brought a sudden jolt of recognition to Bethany that curdled her stomach.

Her fate was exactly the same as the gyrfalcon! Zakr would have her shackled in a protected place, blinded to everything else but serving him, and responding only to his touch. She would become his possession, just as the bird would . . . a slave to her master. Hadn't Zakr himself told her that, like the falcon, she would not want to go free? And already he had built up a compelling need for his stroking, his favour, his being with her!

She had to do something very positive about breaking his power over her as quickly as possible, before he owned her body and soul, before she reached the point of not wanting to live without him. She shivered at the thought. It seemed so extreme, and yet it wasn't. He had only to touch her as he was touching the bird and...

He turned to her with a warm smile which reinforced his power over her to such a dangerous extent that Bethany shivered again in her struggle to raise defences against it.

Zakr's smile turned quizzical. 'The bird still frightens you?'

'No!' It wasn't true, any more than it had been true at the airport. Bethany now understood what she had felt then. It was Zakr who was the falcon, the bird of prey. She and the giant creature on the perch were one and the same...his prize captives.

'I don't like you, Zakr! I never will!' she cried, the words bursting from her lips in a frantic attempt to break free of the power he exerted over her.

His smile was so abruptly wiped out that Bethany stumbled back in fear of her own foolhardiness at blurting out such an offence. Zakr's arm snaked out and caught her, his fingers biting hard as he dragged her into a punishing embrace.

'You have no choice.' His voice was controlled, his face stonily impassive, but his eyes blazed into hers like deadly lasers. 'I will have you, Bethany. And you will love me.'

'No! No!'

In frenzied panic she kicked out at him, and, as her sandalled foot connected with his leg, his grasp on her loosened enough for Bethany to wrench herself away. But, as luck would have it, her foot tangled with the skirt of her long gown and she tumbled forward, barely saving herself from falling flat on her face. Instinctively she twisted her body in a gymnast roll that should have freed her legs enough to scramble to her feet, but Zakr's foot pinned her gown to the concrete floor, and she could not tear it free.

'Let me go!' she screamed.

'Never!' he seethed back at her in a black fury that struck terror in her heart.

He knelt to pick her up, and Bethany hit out wildly, knocking one of his arms away and striking his face. Vice-like fingers closed around her wrists, and Bethany's arms were slammed above her head as Zakr's body came crashing down on top of hers, knocking the breath out of her.

'I will teach you what the truth is, and you will never deny me again,' he cried hoarsely, then cut off any word Bethany might have said by ravaging her mouth with his.

She fought him with all the grim strength she could muster: bucking, writhing, twisting her head from side to side, her whole body striving wildly to escape from his mastery. She would not be subdued. Nor would she surrender to his will again.

But she no sooner tore her mouth from his than he captured it again, barely giving her time to gasp in breath. She didn't know when his need to dominate turned into the passion of sexual arousal, or whether the two were the same, but she was frighteningly aware of his hardening flesh jabbing against her stomach.

He released one of her hands and dragged up her skirt. She beat at him with her fist, thrashed out with the leg he had freed, but he had her other leg pinned under his and her whole body quivered with weakness as she felt him adjust his own clothing. He was going to take her! Right here on the floor of the mews!

He lifted his head as he forcefully repositioned himself over her, and Bethany tried to say no, but her tongue wouldn't work, and her throat was so gravelly dry that it only emitted a weak groan.

He pushed into her without any care or preparation, and Bethany was shamed to realise that the very struggle that had excited him had also affected her. Her muscles contracted around him in welcoming pleasure as he plunged the depths of her womb, and her arms fell limply to her sides, shot through with the now familiar ache that melted the tensile strength she had drawn to its limits in order to keep fighting him.

Her body shuddered its betrayal with his every surging thrust, and he hammered his possession of her until what little will-power she had left shattered into total submission. His climax seemed to be a punctuation of his triumph over her, and when his body sank on to hers, finally drained of its mad need to claim ownership, Bethany did not try to move.

She looked up at the great Greenland gyrfalcon perched above them, and tears filled her eyes. Captives for ever. The only difference was she couldn't soar the skies alone. She needed Zakr to take her with him.

Zakr's harsh breathing gradually subsided. He rolled off her and hunched forward to pull down her skirt. He dragged up his legs, rested his elbows on his knees, and buried his face in his hands for several long moments.

Bethany didn't move. She didn't have a grain of energy left in her. And she was beyond caring what happened to her now.

'I have never done that to a woman. Never in my life.'

The muffled words held an agonised guilt, and Bethany was deeply touched by the intense feeling that throbbed out of them.

'I would never have believed myself capable of such a grievous loss of control,' he continued in hoarse regret. 'I swear to you it will never happen again, Bethany, no matter what the provocation.'

He pushed himself to his feet, keeping his back turned to her as he readjusted his clothing. His reluctance to face her was obvious in the taut squaring of his shoulders before he finally swung around, and even then he did not meet her eyes.

He picked up the cloak that had fallen from his shoulders, then knelt to gently tuck it around her. Very carefully he slid his arms under her shoulders and thighs and lifted her up. He carried her out of the mews and back to the hunting lodge, and not once did he look down at her.

His face was drawn into the sharp austerity of a man doing the heaviest penance of his life, and Bethany slowly realised that his feelings for her were a lot more complex than she had ever imagined. It comforted her to know that she affected him so deeply.

He laid her on the bed, took off her sandals and covered her with a quilt. 'Try to sleep, Bethany,' he urged softly, then left her in a driven haste that spoke all too clearly of a great disturbance of mind.

Bethany wearily closed her eyes. She would not think of it now. She did not understand what had changed between them, but something had. The strange thing was...she didn't mind what Zakr had done. It proved something, but her mind couldn't quite grasp what it was. He had demanded her love...wanted it...needed it. Had she just given it to him?

CHAPTER NINE

BETHANY slept intermittently throughout the night and well into the next morning. Whenever she awoke there was a servant woman sitting by the bed, eager to bring her anything she wanted, or carry out any of her wishes. She was plied with food and drink, helped to the bathroom, fussed over and cosseted as though she were an invalid child.

Zakr did not return, not to see or speak to or touch her. Nor to share the bed with her. Many times Bethany woke in the act of feeling for him beside her, and she was ashamed of the need that his continued absence sharpened.

Was it pride that kept him away? Certainly his violent reaction to her rejection had shaken his self-image. Was he giving himself time to re-establish the ingrained sense of control which was so much a part of his aura of power?

On the other hand, maybe her rejection had cut very deep. She hadn't recanted on her vehement declaration that she didn't like him and never would. Had he let himself believe it? Did he now doubt that she would ever give him the love he insisted upon? Perhaps he was even considering the possibility that he had made a mistake with her.

Bethany breakfasted, bathed and dressed, hoping every minute that Zakr would come striding in to see her. But he didn't come. Nor was there any message from him. Finally in frustration she questioned the woman who seemed to be in charge of all the other servants who tripped in and out.

'What is the sheikh doing today?' she asked casually, pride dictating that she not reveal how much she was churning over his avoidance of her.

'I do not know, my lady,' was the most unhelpful reply.

'Is he here?'

'No, my lady. He is gone. Early this morning.'

Gone? And left her here without a word? Bethany's heart sank. Perhaps he really did think she would spurn him again. If only he had given her the chance to tell him how she felt ... yet, in all truth, Bethany couldn't say that she loved him. Not love in the sense that she imagined love should be: a knowing and understanding and giving to each other.

'I suppose he's gone hunting,' she said on a despondent sigh, thinking of all the empty hours that stretched ahead of her before he would return.

'I do not know, my lady,' came the bland answer.

'Of course you must know!' Bethany snapped impatiently. 'Are the horses gone? The falcons? You must have noticed!'

The woman shook her head, her eyes wide and anxious at Bethany's loss of temper. 'The prince left in the helicopter. That's all I know.'

He could be anywhere, Bethany thought, and sheer panic scrambled her mind for several moments. He could be gone for weeks while she remained imprisoned here. He might forget all about her! Find some other woman who was only too happy to dote on him all the time.

Her sense of loss was so sharp that Bethany gave a groan of anguish, and the sound of her own pain forced her to face up to the truth of the situation. The strength of her need for Zakr appalled her. If she stayed here much longer, her emotional dependence on him could only deepen, and their relationship as it stood could not possibly lead to any lasting happiness for her.

Pride surged over the pain. She would not let him do this to her. She would show him that he couldn't fly off and ignore her, expecting her to wait until he deigned to show her his favour again. She would not be reduced to a slave. Never! She had to escape, not only for her father's sake, but her own. And now was the time to leave, while Zakr was away and she still had enough will-power to break free.

Spurred on by the thought of her father, and anger at Zakr's cavalier treatment of her, Bethany concentrated hard on how best to break the chains of her imprisonment. Her position as the sheikh's mistress surely gave her some authority in the household. She was being waited on hand and foot, pampered in every way. Zakr had shown that even he respected her wishes, and valued her highly, since he had given her the perfume of the Pharaohs. Maybe she could bluff her way out. It was worth a try.

She turned to her attendant with an air of haughty carelessness. 'Well, since the sheikh isn't here, I can wear my own clothes, can't I?' she declared, and strode off to the dressing-room where all her belongings had been stored, along with her new wardrobe of more 'suitable' gowns.

The woman fluttered after her, babbling agitated protests, but Bethany refused to listen to them. She deliberately changed into the khaki slacks and jacket, and jammed on the cloth hat that Zakr had disliked so much.

'I am going for a walk in the grounds,' she announced with all the calm authority of a theatre-sister.

Her attendant's face screwed up with anxiety and she wrung her hands as she spoke. 'You cannot do that, my lady.'

'Oh, yes, I can!' said Bethany, picking up her bag of medical supplies and brushing past the woman with a determined step. And if she found one of Zakr's supply trucks with the ignition keys in it, she would steal it without compunction.

The woman hurried after her, tugging at Bethany's sleeve. 'The sheikh gave orders!' she cried.

Bethany spun on her heel. 'What orders?' she barked.

'You are not to leave this suite of rooms, my lady. Guards are posted at the doors. You must stay here. You will not be allowed to pass. The sheikh...' she swallowed nervously '...he cannot be disobeyed.'

The whole momentum of Bethany's escape idea suddenly lost its steam. Not only had Zakr left her, but he had seen to it that she was imprisoned for the term of his majesty's pleasure. Or displeasure, as the case might be.

Shackled! Just like the falcon. The vivid imagery that had swamped her mind yesterday came back with even more force, making Bethany feel totally helpless. Zakr wouldn't let her go. He would keep her tied to him for ever. And, most horrifying of all, there was a curious peace in that thought. No more struggling, no more wondering about the future...she was here for him.

Bethany shook her head, doing her utmost to wrench herself out of the mesmerising sense of inevitability. She had to flee today, while she still had the strength of mind to do it. But how? With the doors guarded and her room three storeys up from the ground...

The scaffolding! Was it still there? Could she possibly reach it without alerting any guards?

Bethany wandered over to the window. Only a bird could escape from here, Zakr had said, and Bethany fiercely wished she had the falcon's strong wings. The scaffolding was still there, but out of reach from her suite of rooms. She was already turning away in a mood of bleak despair when her gaze caught the ledge that marked the floor level of each storey.

Very casually, so as not to alarm her watch-guard attendant, Bethany opened the window, pulled up a chair, and sat there with her elbows resting on the sill, apparently content to stare out at the view. Was the ledge wide enough for her to edge along it to the scaffolding? If it had been freestanding, she could have done cartwheels along it...no problem at all. But the wall made the balancing very tricky.

One thing was certain. She couldn't tote a bag of medical supplies along that ledge. And she couldn't just drop the bag out of the window from this height. Asking for a rope would certainly raise suspicions, and a couple of sheets tied together would not suffice. Bethany considered the problem for quite some time before she removed the offensive cloth hat and ruffled her hair with her hand.

She smiled at the woman, who had relaxed under Bethany's pose of placid acceptance. 'Are there any ribbons I could use to tie up my hair?' she asked hopefully.

The woman beamed approval at such a feminine request. A whole box of ribbons was brought. Bethany took her time selecting a blue one, then fiddled around with it, eventually tying her long tresses into a ponytail. She asked that the box remain in her room in case she wanted a different ribbon tonight. That request evoked no argument either.

She ate a very light lunch, remarked that she was still tired and wanted to sleep, and finally managed to usher the woman out of the bedroom.

Bethany quickly fetched her handbag from the dressing-room, took off her shoes and socks, stuffed them into the bag, crammed her hat in on top of them, then set to work, tying the end of the largest reel of ribbon to the handles of the two bags she needed.

She used up three reels of ribbon; tying them into a long rope which she then used to lower her bags to the ground below. She wished she could trust her own weight to the makeshift rope, but didn't dare risk it. Steeling her courage to the sticking-point, she carefully lowered herself over the windowsill, keeping a very firm grip on it as her toes felt for the ledge. Then, very slowly, she moved to the end of the window and balanced herself against the wall.

Her heart was hammering fearfully as she let the sill go but, with all the trained instincts of an experienced gymnast, Bethany had judged her balance to perfection. Escape was possible if she kept her concentration. It was now or never!

She called on a lifetime of self-discipline and moved step by precarious step towards the scaffolding. Don't look down, she schooled herself. Just keep going in a steady, unbroken rhythm.

Bethany was almost there when the helicopter broke her intense inner-focus. The noise of its beating propellers seemed to be directly above her, but to lift her head to look would be to invite disaster. Was it Zakr returning? Could he see her? Was he sitting up there watching her?

Bethany fought back wave after wave of panic. The helicopter was probably hovering over the landing-pad on the other side of the lodge. It just sounded close. She had to go on. If it was Zakr returning, he might go up to the bedroom and find her missing. Time could be running out on her.

She could see the scaffolding out of the corner of her eye. Only a couple of more steps. Or if she pushed off the ledge and twisted her body into a sideways leap... Do or die, she told herself in reckless bravado, and leapt.

Her hands caught the pipe crossbar and gripped as she swung her body to lessen the weight-fall.

Elation soared through her heart. She had done it! She swung from bar to bar with effortless grace, and even did a madcap somersault on to the ground.

Only then did she look up to check the helicopter's position. Its tail was just disappearing over the roof. Had it been hovering above her during those critical moments? Impossible to tell, and certainly there was no time to waste.

Bethany sped across the ground, untied her bags, then raced for the sheds where the supply trucks were garaged, praying that any attendants were having an afternoon siesta. Luck favoured her. There didn't seem to be anyone around, and the first truck she checked had its keys dangling from the ignition. She climbed in, pulled on her socks and shoes, tucked her hair up under the hat, and sent up another wild prayer as she tried the motor.

It was just like appropriating P.J.'s jeep. Everything worked perfectly. She trundled the truck out of the shed and made for the gateway to freedom.

Every moment Bethany expected someone to appear and try to stop her. She was very much afraid that one of the soldiers might shoot her tyres as Zakr had done to the jeep. It wasn't until she rounded a stand of palm-trees and the gateway was right in front of her that she understood why there had been no interference in her bid for escape.

The soldiers were all lined up on either side of the road like a guard of honour, rifles at the ready but not aimed at her…yet. Not one of them moved to halt the progress of the truck.

They didn't have to.

Between the two huge gate pillars, blocking any viable passageway, stood the Sheikh of Bayrar, armed only with the formidable power of his personal authority.

Never had Bethany seen him look so fierce or so arrogantly proud in his bearing. He did not raise a hand. He did not speak a word. The black eyes simply bored through the truck's windscreen, straight into Bethany's heart, and not for one moment did her mind even begin to question the challenge he offered her.

She could leave if she wished.

Over his dead body!

With a sigh of hopeless defeat, Bethany applied the brakes and switched off the engine. Zakr's look of scorn whipped across the remaining space at her. It almost seemed as if he would have preferred her to kill him. Why wasn't he exulting that he had won over her... yet again? Would she ever understand this complex man?

Tears blurred her eyes and Bethany dropped her head on to the steering wheel. There was nowhere to go. She was his prisoner again. She always would be. She simply couldn't be as ruthless as he was.

The truck door was opened. She looked up, expecting to face Zakr's wrath, but it was a soldier who stood there, motioning her out. Zakr still hadn't moved. Bethany tried to muster some dignity, but she stumbled as she alighted, and the soldier grasped her arm to steady her. He did not let her go. Another soldier fell in beside her, taking her other arm, and she was ignominiously escorted back to the bedroom on the third floor.

One of the soldiers remained on sentry at the window through which she had escaped. There could be no doubt now that Zakr had seen her from the helicopter. He had simply given her enough rope with which to hang herself. It was a long, agonising hour before he made his appearance on the scene, and even then his austere countenance was a study of tightly controlled fury.

Bethany hardly dared to face him. The tension emanating from him was enough to choke every nerve in her body. The soldier and servants were dismissed with a rifle-snap of his fingers. Bethany steeled herself to meet and hold the blazing black gaze as doors closed them in alone together.

'Your stupidity is only exceeded by the madness of your bravery!'

The whiplash of his words stung Bethany into vehement retort. 'You're not going to cage me, Zakr. I'm not so stupid as to want to spend the rest of my life incarcerated here as your captive.'

Rage was in every stalking step as he crossed the space between them. His hands closed around Bethany's upper arms and bit as he shook her violently. 'You risked the life of my son!'

Defiance burned off her tongue. 'You don't even know if I'm pregnant.'

'You carry my son!' he thundered.

'And what about my father?' Bethany yelled back. 'You don't care about him! I had to go. And I'll keep going until I find him! You can be as much of a tyrannical brute to me as you like, but you can't make me forget why I came here.'

He picked his hands off her and clenched them at his sides. His whole body stiffened into towering dignity. He spoke with grim-faced pride. 'You have nothing to fear from me, Bethany Lyon McGregor. I shall never force myself on you again. I have only detained you now in order to inform you that your father is alive.'

'My father!' Shock and wild, dizzying hope chased every other thought out of her head. She looked up at Zakr in breathless appeal, wanting . . . needing to know more.

The black eyes glared hatred at her. 'Did I not say I would take care of everything for you? One of my scouting party located him yesterday afternoon. He is being held captive by the Marxist guerrillas in one of their strongholds.'

His scouting party! He had been referring to her father when he had said it was best to know where to hunt. 'Why didn't you tell me?' she cried plaintively.

His face stiffened further. 'For what purpose? It would have been cruel to raise your hopes when it was virtually a certainty that your father had been killed.'

'But he's alive! He's alive!' Bethany crowed joyously, and in a fervour of gratitude for Zakr's generous pursuit of her own mission, she threw her arms around him. Her huge blue eyes sparkled like sunlight on water and her ecstatic smile would have rewarded a thousand men . . . but not Prince Zakr Tahnun Sadiq.

He snatched her hands down from his neck and stepped back, almost flinging her arms away from him. Intense pain flashed briefly from his eyes and was gone, replaced with the dark fire of deeply wounded pride.

'There is most of the Shihuh tribe as well. What I do is for them. If I help your father, it is incidental. I have no reason to feel otherwise when you treat me so...contemptuously.'

'I only wanted to thank you,' Bethany said in soft appeasement, chastened by the realisation that he had cared about her feelings.

'Keep the love you bear your father to yourself!' he snarled at her. 'For *him* you would do anything! And I am nothing to you.'

The sheer venom of his speech showed the depth of the hurt she had unwittingly inflicted. 'That's not true,' Bethany whispered.

'Is it not?' he mocked savagely. 'You risked your life for him! You risked the life of our child for him! You struck fear into my heart that has never been there before. But that is of no concern to you. Your concern is all for your father.'

'If you had only told me what you were doing...' Bethany pleaded.

He made a sharp, contemptuous gesture. 'Do you think I would want you to stay with me for the sake of your father?'

He strode to the door, then turned one last blistering look at her. 'Tomorrow I will bring him back to you. Then you may both go. And never return to my country. I do not need you in my life, Bethany Lyon McGregor. And I will not.'

And on that scathing note he left. Bethany sagged on to the bed, feeling as though her life's blood had been drained out of her.

It was what she wanted, wasn't it? For Zakr to release her... to get her father back... go home. She had rejected Zakr. Why should it distress her so much that he had just rejected her? She was free of him.

Except she didn't feel free. She felt like an outcast, craving for what could never be hers again. And not all the positive thinking she forced through her mind could lift the terrible weight of depression from her heart.

He had come back and she was his captive again. It made no difference that she was no longer shackled in a physical sense. Somehow she had become linked to him in a far more intangible way. Bethany knew with bleak certainty that she would never forget Zakr Tahnun Sadiq as long as she lived.

Hours passed, but Bethany was barely aware of the passage of time. She noticed grimly that the woman-servant she had deceived this afternoon was no longer appointed to her service. Other women fluttered around, urging her into a bath, then seeing she was properly groomed and dressed in one of the exotic caftans.

Bethany considered it all a waste of time—Zakr had no intention of seeing her tonight—but she did not have the heart to upset anyone else by making some useless stand.

As she expected, there was no invitation to dine with Zakr. A meal was brought to her room.

She was astonished when a summons did actually come. A woman came hurrying into the room and bowed a greeting. 'The Prince commands your presence, my lady. If you will please follow me...'

It did not enter Bethany's mind to refuse. Her pulse raced along in agitated leaps as she stood up and accompanied the woman. She couldn't imagine what Zakr might want with her, but she hoped there would be an opportunity to make peace with him. Self-honesty forced her to deride that thought. It wasn't peace she wanted with him. At least...not that kind of peace.

However, any hopes of a reconciliation were abruptly squashed the moment she entered the room where they had shared their first meal.

Zakr was not alone. There were other men with him, and Bethany was startled to recognise Abdul, her driver, as one of them. They were not seated at the round table, but on the chaise-longues.

The men rose as Bethany was ushered towards them. All of them except Zakr. He waved a careless invitation for her to sit next to him.

His manner seemed relaxed, his expression unreadable. He did not bother introducing her to his companions. They resumed their seats after Bethany had settled stiffly at the end of Zakr's chaise-longue.

'We are just about to enjoy some entertainment,' he informed her. 'I thought it might distract you from your worries.'

Was there the tiniest bit of acid edging those soft words? Something caused her heart to contract. Underneath Zakr's very controlled exterior, she sensed the boiling anger of a furnace about to explode.

'That's very kind of you. Thank you,' she murmured, conscious of a burning sensation in her own cheeks. She was so close to him, yet so far away.

Zakr clapped his hands and the orchestra on the stage began to play eastern music with which Bethany was unfamiliar. Tonight there was no backing curtain to the shower of golden beads in front of the stage. To Bethany's acute displeasure, a very curvaceous belly-dancer stepped through the bead-curtain and down on to the clear carpet square in front of the stage.

She was good at shimmying her body around to the music. Too damned good! Bethany caught the smile on Zakr's lips out of the corner of her eye and felt like clawing his eyes out. The belly-dancer was smiling at him too, and flirting with her kohl-lined sloe eyes.

Bethany sat through five dance acts, and the struggle to keep calm and composed was a losing battle. Zakr had deliberately engineered this show to demonstrate that he didn't need her, that he could have the pick of any number of luscious, sexy women. The blatant invitation in their eyes was all too obvious.

He didn't give a damn about her or what she felt any more. He was making sure she knew that he wouldn't miss her after she had gone. Whatever he had felt for her was finished.

'Excellent dancing, don't you think?' he taunted softly as the fifth body bountiful departed off-stage.

'Excellent,' agreed Bethany. 'Given their limitations,' she added, unable to stop herself from saying the obvious truth.

'What limitations?' he asked derisively.

Bethany shrugged. 'Acres of flesh shaking itself in the same patterns *ad infinitum*. Personally, I find it all rather boring. I can do better than that.'

'You?' He gave a mocking chuckle. 'These women are born to dance. Trained from infancy. And yet you can match them?'

'If I couldn't do better than that, I'd hang up my gymnast shoes,' Bethany retorted with all the sting of a highly irritated wasp. She was fiercely jealous of the belly-dancers, jealous that Zakr could even find any small pleasure in looking at another woman, let alone want one.

There was a pause, and Bethany, whose pride had forbade her to look at him, was drawn against her will to meet his eyes. They were half shuttered against her, but the probing gleam of those narrowed black slits commanded her full attention.

'You did not tell me you were a gymnast,' he said quietly.

'You did not tell me you would search for my father,' she retorted. 'I don't like being left in the dark either!'

'It is not a woman's place . . .'

'I will not be slotted into your idea of a woman's place,' Bethany said fiercely. 'I'm me!'

His mouth twitched into that half-smile that always confused Bethany. 'You are arguing with me again,' he observed drily. 'Perhaps it is time you proved one of your arguments, Bethany Lyon McGregor. Dance for me.'

'I'll do that!' Bethany snapped, and rose immediately to her feet. 'Please excuse me while I change into something more suitable.'

She barely waited for his nod of permission. Adrenalin was pumping through her veins at a faster rate than it had ever done at competitions. She would show him! She would knock his eyes out! And he would forget all about those damnably erotic belly-dancers!

Fifteen minutes later she returned, still seething with emotions that she vaguely recognised were way out of control. Yet she'd be damned if she would leave Zakr without stamping an impression on him that would last all his life! He would remember her! To his dying day he would remember her!

Zakr was alone. The other men had gone, and the curtain had been pulled across the stage. Bethany was glad. She only wanted to perform for him. Not that anything would have stopped her, but any inhibitions she might have had in front of other men were instantly wiped out.

'What music would you like?' Zakr asked with an air of disinterest.

'Can your orchestra play the theme music from "Chariots of Fire"?' she challenged.

'There should be a disc,' he replied carelessly, and clapped his hands.

A man poked his head through the curtain and Zakr gave the order. Bethany had been prepared to do her floor routine without music, but she was secretly thrilled that the stage was apparently equipped with a hi-fi system.

'You choose strange music for dancing,' Zakr observed with a faint note of curiosity.

Bethany smiled and discarded her robe, revealing the blue leotard that fitted her like a second skin. Zakr's hooded eyes flew wide open in surprise, and Bethany positively preened her body into her opening stance. Sheer diabolical wantonness pumped through her, obliterating everything but the need to excite this man to the point where he could not possibly resist her. She would make him want her so much that no pride or power could stop him from showing it.

With an arrogant little flick of her wrist, she released the roll of ribbon she held and its length floated on to the floor. Her eyes taunted him openly in the moment before the music began, and then she used her body with an inspired skill that showed Zakr exactly what he would be missing if he ever thought he could prefer those over-blown belly-dancers to her.

She twirled the ribbon into teasing life around her as she mixed the sensuous grace of ballet with the sinuous athleticism of gymnastic exercises. Every movement was calculated to show her body off in some emphatic way, and she didn't care how provocatively sexual she was in front of Zakr. His occasional gasps of disbelief exhilarated Bethany further, exciting her into excessive sensuality.

She exulted in doing everything possible to taunt and excite him: swaying her body in front of him, undulating with a boneless grace that exposed every curve of her femininity. Each movement swept smoothly into the next, building excitement to a triumphant climax that brought Zakr to his feet.

Bethany held her final pose for several moments after the music ended, her legs extended in a full split, her head tilted back, her back arched, her chest heaving. She exulted at the quick rise and fall of Zakr's torso, the tight clench of the hands, the feverish glint of desire in his eyes as he stared down at her. When she moved, he jerked forward, as if breaking out of a trance. She pushed herself upright and was instantly caught in his embrace.

His hands strained her body closer to his as he rained passionate kisses over her face and hair. 'Do not deny me, Bethany,' he pleaded. 'Not now...one last time...that is all I ask.'

And he took her mouth with a fierce hunger that she answered just as fiercely. There was no stopping the need that clawed through her, nor any quelling of her greed for every expression of his need for her.

She had succeeded.

Zakr was out of control.

Beyond himself with desperate need.

Bethany revelled in his passion for her, and gave it back to him with a reckless abandonment that ignored tomorrow and all the other days ahead of them. There was only now...and now was an ecstatic madness that demanded every last grain of satisfaction and fulfilment.

CHAPTER TEN

BETHANY was not locked up. No guards stood at the doors to prevent her from leaving. She was free to go wherever she liked, whenever she liked. Yet she might as well have been bound hand and foot. Zakr had gone but when . . . or if . . . he returned, it would be with her father.

How dangerous was this rescue mission? What if her father . . . if Zakr . . . was injured or killed? Someone was sure to be hurt if there was fighting, and Bethany could not fool herself that the Marxist guerillas would give their prisoners up without some force being applied. Armed force!

Bethany wanted her father back safe and sound. Of course she did! But Zakr . . . he was putting himself at risk for her sake! She knew he was, even though he had denied it. It wasn't necessary for him to lead his task-force. He was doing it because . . . out of pride, or love?

Bethany wished she knew. She castigated herself for not asking him last night when she'd had the chance. She hadn't even asked him how he proposed to get her father out of the guerrilla stronghold. They hadn't spoken at all, not sorted out a damned thing! They had simply made insatiable demands on each other until Bethany had fallen asleep in his arms.

And he had left without waking her. It was the sound of the helicopter departing that had torn her out of sleep, and it had still been dark. Before dawn. And every hour that had passed since then increased Bethany's frantic worrying. It was almost noon! Where was he now? What was happening? How dangerous was it?

'One last time...' The words that had burst from him in his desperate need for her kept echoing through Bethany's mind. What had Zakr meant by them? Did they mean that he still intended to let her go as she had demanded, despite what he himself wanted? Or had he anticipated not living through today?

Bethany tried to shake off the tortured thoughts. She got out her medical supplies and checked them through. If her father had been imprisoned for all these weeks, he could be ill, needing urgent treatment. Zakr would be all right. Nothing could beat him when he made up his mind. He could probably take that stronghold by will-power alone!

But he hadn't been able to resist her, Bethany reminded herself with intense satisfaction. For several moments she exulted in the memory of last night's mad passion, but then her own chaotic emotions forced her to reappraise what she felt for him.

However crazy it was, she wanted that arrogant, autocratic man, and she didn't really want to leave him at all. But she wouldn't put up with being regarded as little more than a slave to his wishes. He had to recognise that she had a will, too. If he could bring himself to regard her as ... well, not exactly as an equal...but at least someone worthy of being taken into his confidence, then Bethany felt she could be very happy with him. Ecstatically happy.

A deep sigh wiped the silly smile off her face. How could she consider a future with him? It wouldn't work. She was stupid for even thinking it might. She didn't know the first thing about mixing in his kind of society, or even if he would allow her to mix. Here she was, installed in his hunting lodge...the falcon's mistress.

But if she gave him a son... She wondered if she was pregnant, as Zakr said.

The noise of the rotating blades of the helicopter beating through the air snapped Bethany out of her reverie. She ran to the window and caught a glimpse of it as it passed. There was no doubt that Zakr was in it, but what of her father?

Bethany ran out of the room and raced down the stairs, cursing herself for not being out at the landing-pad, waiting for them.

Zakr was already at the entrance to the huge reception room when she reached the ground floor. He was closely flanked by two grim-faced men, and Zakr's face was more tautly austere than Bethany had ever seen it.

Fear choked her and her hand flew up to her throat. 'My...father?' she forced out, her mind screaming a desperate denial of the answer which seemed written on their faces.

Zakr moved stiffly towards her, as if pushing his legs forward strained his will-power to the limit. His arms lifted, his hands falling heavily on

Bethany's shoulders. His eyes . . . his eyes were sick with pain!

'We have found your father. He is unharmed.'

Relief washed through her, yet the sense that something was terribly wrong fretted her mind. 'Where is he?' she asked shakily.

'He will be brought here tomorrow. As soon as all the wounded have been attended to and transport is available. He is safe, Bethany. . .' The sick eyes bored into hers, begging, commanding. 'And now you must help me protect my people.'

She shook her head in bewilderment. 'I don't understand, Zakr. What can I do?'

'Listen to me closely, Bethany. And for once, don't argue. You have to do exactly as I tell you. It is the only way.' He paused to draw breath, and winced from the effort. 'To get your father back, we have created a somewhat small international incident. But it has the potential to blow up into something bigger. We have to avert that happening.'

'How? Why?' The questions burst off her tongue.

'Listen!' he bit out through clenched teeth, and again drew a painful breath.

Bethany bit her lips, angry with herself for the impulsive outburst. Zakr's whole countenance and bearing impressed on her that what he had to say was vitally important. And urgent.

The sound of another helicopter coming in caused him to pause for another few moments. There was a commotion around them, servants and soldiers making ready for something, but Bethany ignored them. Zakr needed her, in a different way from his need of last night, but the need was deep and even more desperate.

'Bethany...' It was a plea that struck straight at her heart. 'My soldiers had to cross our border to get to the guerrillas responsible for the imprisonment of your father and the Shihuh tribe. It was a forced labour camp. The prisoners were being used to build up defences. What we did... we had to do to rescue them.'

He shook his head, as if forcing enough concentration to go on. 'To avert open warfare now, we have to gain sympathy for our cause. And so, you must marry me, Bethany. There is no other choice. It is the only thing that will suffice. If you are my wife...'

His eyes clouded for a moment, and then sharpened again, probing hers for the necessary acquiescence. 'I will divorce you later—if you wish. But don't argue now, Bethany.'

'I won't,' she promised softly, automatically responding to his need. Her hand lifted instinctively to slide up his chest and he caught it hard, his arm trembling as his fingers closed tightly around hers.

'I beg you... do not touch me,' he cried in a hoarse whisper.

And she knew then. He was terribly hurt. She couldn't see where. With his cloak draped around his shoulders, whatever injury he had was not obvious, but Bethany's intuition told her it was grievous.

'Zakr, let me help you,' she pleaded.

He managed a faint half-smile. 'Marry me.'

'Yes, of course I will,' she tossed off impatiently. 'But . . .'

His eyes closed and his body started to sag forward. His hands clutched at her convulsively, and Bethany steeled herself to take the brunt of his weight.

'For God's sake, Zakr! You've got to lie down. Let me . . .'

'No!' He rallied his life-force again. 'Abdul!' he cried, and the man rushed forward. 'Support me. What is keeping them? We must proceed!'

'They are coming, sire. Everything is ready.'

A flurry of people entered the reception room, several of them in some kind of ceremonial dress, others looking very official with their sober demeanour.

'My lady, you are ready?' Abdul asked anxiously.

Bethany suddenly grasped that a marriage service was to take place now! 'Abdul, he needs treatment! Can't this wait?'

The old man shook his head. 'It is his will.'

And Zakr had asked her, begged her not to argue. She heaved a deep, frightened sigh and nodded. Very gently, she curled her arm around Zakr's and faced the men who were obviously some kind of priests.

The marriage service began. Bethany was too dazed to follow it. She made the responses that were required of her. Zakr made his in a weak, strained voice. She prayed desperately for it to be over. She hurriedly scrawled her signature on a document. Zakr laboured shakily over his.

'It is done,' he breathed hoarsely. 'See that it is recorded for this day.'

He half turned to Bethany, a strange, weary triumph flicking into his eyes before they dulled. He toppled forward, and Bethany and Abdul caught him. Between them they eased him to the floor.

'Where is he hurt?' Bethany demanded fiercely.

'A wound in the chest,' Abdul answered, flicking her a sharp look. 'Shrapnel! There is nothing we can do.'

'Like hell there isn't!' Bethany muttered. She threw back the cloak and sucked in her breath as she saw the field-dressing underneath the torn *abba*. Dear God! It was near his heart! Her eyes flew in alarm to the man kneeling across from her. 'He needs a doctor! Why didn't you take him to the hospital?'

'It is forbidden. The sheikh commanded it. Until all the wounded have been treated, no doctor is allowed to touch him.'

'How long will that be?' Bethany snapped out in horror at the headstrong foolhardiness of the man she had just married.

The old man spread his hands in hopeless uncertainty. 'Hours. Days. A long time. It is the will of Allah.'

'This can't wait for days!'

Abdul shook his head. 'It is the sheikh's will. We cannot disobey him.'

A fury of frustration burned through Bethany. 'I am not going to let him die,' she stated in grim defiance of Abdul's fatalistic attitude.

She snatched the gold *agal* from its scabbard at Zakr's waist. The flash of the wickedly curved knife brought a concerted gasp from the onlookers, but Bethany didn't hesitate. The blade was razor-sharp and she quickly cut a long opening in the *abba*, making the chest-wound easily accessible.

She gently removed the dressing. The shrapnel wound was deep and jagged, dirty, and still bleeding! 'It has to be cleaned and stitched,' she stated categorically.

Again Abdul made a helpless gesture of resignation.

'If you won't bring a doctor to him, I'll do it myself,' she declared grimly. Her gaze flashed purposefully around the fear-paralysed onlookers, picking out the women servants she recognised and rapping out her orders in a voice that emulated Matron Vaughan's.

'You! Bring me my bag of medical supplies! You! We must have boiling water...' She rattled off everything that was necessary for the task she had set herself, then turned back to Abdul. 'You...you must fly to the hospital and bring me back plasma. Your sheikh is in shock and must have it to survive. And don't tell me you can't do it!' she added scornfully.

Nobody moved...whether from shock or fear of doing the wrong thing Bethany did not know, but panic was beginning to claw through her stomach when Zakr spoke, his voice weak but still carrying the ingrained ring of authority.

'Obey my wife...in all things...except those I have explicitly forbidden.'

To Bethany's intense relief, people jerked into action. She bent over Zakr, eyes anxiously beseeching his. 'Please, Zakr, change your mind. Let me take you to a hospital and a doctor.'

His face sheened with sweat from the pain and he slowly shook his head. 'I place my fate...in your hands.'

'I'll hurt you, Zakr. You need anaesthetic. You need...'

'Only you.'

'No, please...'

'Bethany...' His eyes opened and slowly focused on hers, gathering an intensity of purpose that burned into her soul. 'If you carry my son...my heir...my people need him.'

'I'll stay, Zakr. I promise you I won't leave.'

A sigh whispered from faintly curved lips as he lost consciousness again.

Tears blurred Bethany's eyes, and she savagely rubbed them away. He was not going to die. She wouldn't let him. And this was no time to be giving into the emotions raging through her.

Clean sheets and pillows were brought. Bethany ordered that one sheet be spread out on the flat table that had been carried in, and the sheikh be lifted on to it. She used the pillows to prop Zakr at the right angle for her to work on him. The medical supplies were handed to her and Bethany was intensely grateful that Matron Vaughan had insisted on her taking anything that could be used in any conceivable emergency.

Her hand shook a little as she filled a syringe with morphine. 'This is to lessen the pain, Zakr,' she said, not knowing if he could hear her, but needing to calm herself into the discipline that was absolutely essential if she was to do what was necessary.

He did not answer her, nor did he react when she inserted the needle. Bethany waited ten minutes for the drug to take effect, then gave him a shot of Pethedine as well.

She opened the packet of surgical gloves and pulled them on. The instruments she would use were packed in sterilised plastic envelopes. If she needed to re-use them they could be plunged into boiling water for sterilisation.

Bethany took several deep breaths, sent up a brief prayer that all would go well, then started probing the wound. Pieces of metal had scattered off the rib-bone in all directions. She used saline solution to irrigate the wound while she removed every piece of foreign matter she could find; sand and dirt included. An X-ray machine was badly needed. She could feel anxiety building up in her as she checked and double-checked that everything that might cause infection had been removed. She could find nothing more.

Her hands started to tremble again as she dropped the surgical instrument back into the water. 'I've done my best, Zakr,' she said, needing to draw confidence from the spoken words.

She clenched and unclenched her hands several times, then started sewing up the broken tissues, using the meticulous surgeon's knot that Dr Hong had taught. It was a long, tedious job drawing the wounded edges back together. Abdul arrived back with the plasma. She had to set up a makeshift drip. Zakr's unconscious body became restless. Morphine was no substitute for a muscle-relaxing anaesthetic.

She ordered people to hold him still. She spread Sulphonamide powder throughout the wound and gave him an injection of Keflin to help combat infection, then inserted the last stitches. There was nothing more she could do.

Bethany stared down at her work with an odd sense of disbelief. How on earth had she had the courage to do all that? And it didn't look too bad. Not bad at all. Suddenly her legs felt very wobbly, and the tears she had kept at bay for so long surged into her eyes. She half blundered to the closest chair and sat down, shaking all over.

'My lady, is there anything more we should do?'

The low, gravelly voice told her it was Abdul. Bethany blinked hard and tried to regather concentration. She swept a tired, blurry look around the room and found everyone watching her with something like awe. With a weird, tingly feeling she recalled that Zakr had placed his authority in her hands. Absolute authority. Her word was law. And they were all waiting for some direction from her.

Zakr needed a doctor, and Bethany silently determined that when the time came that he would accept a doctor's care, he would have the very best. Assuming her most authoritative voice, she gave directions on how to get in touch with St Vincent's Hospital in Sydney. Dr Hong and his team were to be sent to Rhafhar. The need here was too great to count the cost; she had to have him. And Prince Zakr would pay for it.

Next she ordered a door to be brought. It was the most suitable thing she could think of for transporting Zakr to her bedroom. She supervised the whole operation, saw to Zakr's undressing, then sat by the bedside, willing him back to good health.

He grew restless and feverish. Bethany began the long, slow ritual of bathing his forehead and hands, down his face and body, over and over again. She murmured soothing words to him, words that she didn't even realise were revealing expressions of love. All she knew was that she needed him to live for her.

Bethany was not aware of any noise behind her, but some sixth sense alerted her to some new element in the room. It drew her attention from Zakr. She turned abruptly, aggression charging through her heart, ready to do battle with anything in order to protect her patient.

The aggression drained into pained shock at first sight of the man who stood there, drinking her in with a suspicion of moisture in his tired blue eyes. His tall frame looked like a bag of bones, his craggy face gaunt, his body emaciated, the once red hair now totally grey.

'Daddy!'

It was a breath of protest, relief, longing, and all the love she had felt for him since she was a babe in arms.

Then she was on her feet and running. He held out his arms to her and she flung her own around him, hugging him, laughing, crying. 'I knew you weren't dead. I knew you wouldn't die on me. Not if you could help it.' She beamed up at him, sunshine through water. 'Not my Dad.'

He smiled, his love and pride in her illuminated in his tear-filled eyes. 'And I knew you would come for me, my fearless daughter.' The thick emotion broke into a dry little chuckle. 'Though how you managed to arrange a full-scale assault...'

'Zakr did that, Dad,' she assured him hastily. 'I only found your message in the cave.'

'Good bit of art-work, wasn't it?' He gave her one of his old teasing grins.

It made his face look even more gaunt, but Bethany grinned back. 'Pretty rotten, actually. It's just as well I'm a very convincing interpreter.'

He laughed and hugged her again. Bethany could feel his projecting bones and realised she had two nursing cases on her hands. Whatever Doug McGregor had been through since he had disappeared, it had to have been a terrible ordeal to bring him to such a state.

'How did you get here so soon?' she asked brightly, intuitively knowing that he wouldn't want her to fuss over his condition...not yet. 'Zakr said it would be a day or two.'

He shrugged. 'An order came through that I should be brought here by helicopter. I was met by an old Arab who seemed to have the idea that you were the incumbent ruler until Prince Zakr says otherwise.' His eyes glinted with amusement. 'I don't know how you managed that, Bethany, but...'

The total lack of responding amusement in his daughter's eyes gave him pause for thought. 'Bethany, what have you done?' he asked sharply.

She sighed, hoping he would not find it too difficult to understand. 'Zakr and I are married, Dad. And since I'm his wife, naturally I'm in a position of some authority, so...'

'Married!' Incredulity moved swiftly to horror. 'Bethany, surely you knew I would never have expected such a...a sacrifice from you. Good God! I would rather have...'

Her hand swiftly rose to silence his agonising and her eyes begged him to listen and believe. The truth burst from her heart and there was no more uncertainty...no doubt at all.

'I love him, Dad. I didn't marry him for you. I married him because...' It really had nothing to do with international incidents at all, so there wasn't any point in mentioning that side-effect. '...because I want to be his wife.'

He stared at her, struggling to assimilate what she was telling him. His eyes darted to the man in the bed. 'How badly hurt is he?'

Bethany's eyes clouded with worry. 'Bad. He took some shrapnel near his heart. I had to operate, Dad. He refused to have a doctor.'

Anxiety creased her father's brow. 'Bethany, that was a hell of a risk to take. What if he dies?'

'My wife...tells me...I must not die. So I will not.'

'Zakr!' Bethany spun out of her father's embrace and raced to the bedside, picking up the limp hand closest to her and squeezing it in an excess of spilling emotion. 'Oh, Zakr! Are you in terrible pain?'

The black eyes gleamed out under heavy lids. 'You love me, Bethany?'

Tears trembled on her thick lashes. 'I don't want to live without you, Zakr,' she pleaded.

His mouth curved its half-smile. 'Then I am content . . . with pain.'

His eyes closed, but his fingers curled tightly around hers and Bethany lifted them to her mouth and kissed them over and over in an uninhibited release of emotion.

At the foot of the bed, Douglas MacArthur McGregor looked on, shaking his head in dazed wonderment. His daughter . . . and Prince Zakr Tahnun Sadiq! He still hadn't succeeded in tracing the origins of the blue-eyed Shihuh tribe, but he thought in some bemusement that if the next Sheikh of Bayrar was blue-eyed, there would be no problem at all in tracing his genes back to the McGregor clan!

The motto he had printed in the cave ran through his mind—*S'rioghal mo dhream*. Royal is my blood! And so it was, he thought with satisfaction. So it was!

CHAPTER ELEVEN

ZAKR was not a good patient. Bethany got him safely through the first night with a mixture of scolding and a lot of loving. The very next day he was demanding to see his ministers, insisting that he had to know what repercussions were ensuing from yesterday's assault. Only the most dire threats from her kept him in bed.

There was a great deal of traffic in and out of the hunting lodge that day. When Bethany was absolutely certain that Zakr was behaving himself, she appointed Abdul as guardian of the wound, with strict instructions on how much activity his sheikh was allowed. Which was none. Then, with a more easy mind, she went in search of her father.

She found him down in the reception-room, watching the comings and goings with great interest and chatting with P.J. Weatherly. The white-haired archaeologist arched his eyebrows and shook his head at Bethany the moment he caught sight of her. She offered him an appeasing smile as she approached.

'You, young lady, have a lot to answer for,' he drawled, climbing to his feet with a big grin on his face. He took her hand warmly, and Bethany knew she had been forgiven her trespasses, but she apologised anyway.

'I am sorry about the jeep, P.J. You got it back safely and in full repair?'

The eyebrows shot down into a puzzled frown. 'It was delivered back, yes. But what repair did it need? Don't tell me you had an accident.'

'Not exactly,' Bethany said with a rueful grimace. 'Zakr shot the back tyres out.'

'He did what?' her father squawked. 'With you driving, Bethany?'

She sighed and sat down with them. 'Well, Dad, you've got to understand about Zakr. He's a great hunter and when he aims at something he gets it. Also, he's not used to being disobeyed and he doesn't like it very much. But you're not to worry, because I'm getting to know how to handle that,' she added, and the self-satisfied little smile on her lips struck both men into understanding silence for several rather awed moments.

'The power of a woman,' her father muttered with a roll of his eyes at P.J.

'Seems to me you should be thankful for it, Doug,' P.J. retorted drily.

'Dad, you really should be in bed,' Bethany put in, her voice full of concern.

'Nonsense. Fit as a fiddle. You get a lot of exercise in a labour camp.'

'You're a bit thin on it, Doug,' P.J. observed helpfully.

'And you need a thorough medical check,' Bethany added, her eyes boring in to her wayward father's.

'Later,' he agreed. 'But since this is the first real opportunity we've had to talk—and P.J. shares my own avid curiosity—I insist that you do a little explaining, Bethany. You can start with how you came to arrive at P.J.'s site in the sheikh's limousine.'

It was plain that he wasn't going to co-operate with her concern over his health unless she did explain the situation, so Bethany resigned herself to the task. Her agile mind had to keep flitting ahead to edit out the more personal parts of the story. She felt it was wiser to present Zakr in the best possible light, so she didn't mention her escape bid from the hunting lodge, nor the little matter of their separate methods of seduction.

'He really is the most marvellous man, Dad,' she finished with convincing fervour.

P.J. shook his head in bemusement. 'It's a hard country, Bethany. I don't know how you're going to cope.'

Douglas MacArthur McGregor swelled with paternal pride. 'P.J., when my daughter makes up her mind to cope with something, she copes.'

'Ah, yes!' The shake of the head turned into a judicious nod. 'I can see that. Quite right, Doug. Nothing to worry about, is there?'

But there was, as far as Bethany was concerned. She wasn't at all sure that Zakr's will-power could fight off infection if she had missed any pieces of metal in that dreadful wound; and she suspected that her father was far from being as fit as a fiddle.

She plied them both with medications, but neither of them proved as co-operative as she thought they ought to be. Indeed, the next day Zakr insisted they all be transported to the palace, and there was no stopping him. Bethany had to admit that his recovery rate was little short of miraculous. She even began to wonder if he could force his tissues to heal just by the power of his mind.

Bethany had thought the hunting lodge fantastic enough in its interior decoration, but the palace was positively mind-boggling. Its exterior was built of alternate courses of yellow and black stone, and the walls of the interior were a blaze of marble, gold and mother-of-pearl mosaic. The woodwork was magnificently carved and painted; the windows were set with brilliant-coloured glass; and all the floors were executed in imported marbles.

Zakr's two young daughters were brought to meet her. They were quiet, grave little girls, very shy and obviously in much awe of Bethany. At four and six years of age, they had no experience of people outside their own country, and they could not tear their gaze from their new stepmother's cloud of apricot-gold hair.

'I hope they will soon get used to me,' she sighed to Zakr when the children were led away.

'It is not easy,' he muttered, disgruntled by her refusal to get into bed with him.

Her grimace was full of irony. Bethany found it difficult enough to fight her own desires, let alone ward off his. 'It's not easy for me either, Zakr.'

'Good!' he said unsympathetically. 'It is only right that you should suffer, too.'

It was a great relief to Bethany when Dr Hong arrived the following day. Certainly Zakr was no longer feverish and did not show any signs of infection from his wound, but the responsibility for his well-being had been a very heavy burden on her heart. She couldn't bear to be present during his examination, but it was just as nerve-racking waiting for the specialist's definitive opinion.

Had she done some terrible damage in her amateur operation? Would Zakr need further surgery? When Dr Hong finally returned to her with the X-ray results, Bethany was almost ready to leap down his throat to get at the truth.

'Well?' she prompted sharply. As respectful as she was supposed to be to such an illustrious surgeon as Dr Hong, her anxiety over Zakr's welfare demanded an immediate answer.

'Nothing there. You made a clean sweep.' He handed her the X-ray in confirmation of his judgement. 'You did a remarkable job, Sister McGregor. Or...uh...' His mouth pursed in quizzical bemusement. 'What should I call you now?'

'Sister will do just fine,' Bethany replied carelessly. 'You're sure he's healing right?'

'Give him a little time,' the little Chinese doctor said in gentle reprimand for her impatience. 'What I recommend now is what the greatest doctors in the world have been practising for over two thousand years...'

He paused, and Bethany frowned at the little smile that was playing on his mouth. 'And what's that?' she almost snapped, unable to stop worrying.

The smile turned into a full-blown grin. 'A period of masterly inactivity while nature does what we can't.'

'Oh!' Relief swept through her and, as she thought about having Zakr exactly where she could find him for some time to come, a smile curved her own lips. 'And my father?'

'The same. Plus a steady diet of good nutritious food. He really has a remarkably strong constitution for a man of his age.'

Bethany heaved a sigh and cast a speculative look at the man she had ordered to be flown here at astronomical cost. 'Dr Hong, I do appreciate your coming all this way at such short notice...'

He chuckled. 'I got the feeling that I was not at liberty to refuse, Sister McGregor. However, the donation for our research programme certainly made the trip worth while. And I must confess it is extremely diverting to find my best theatre-assistant running a country.'

'Not exactly running it,' Bethany corrected rue-fully. 'In fact, since Zakr doesn't need your skills, it's a bit difficult for me to justify sending for you, Dr Hong. But since you're here, would you take a look at the soldiers who were wounded while rescuing my father? They have been treated, but...just a check?'

'I take your point,' he said drily.

'Oh, good!' Bethany breathed in happy satisfaction. 'I'll take you to the hospital myself and clear the way.'

On the principle that Zakr should not be agitated in any way, Bethany did not inform him of her proposed trip to the hospital. However, what she saw there required very serious discussion which she felt could not be postponed. Indeed, it was a case of taking the bull by the horns without any prevarication. But she did wait until Zakr had been mellowed somewhat by a great deal of loving care.

'I went to the hospital with Dr Hong this afternoon,' she stated bluntly. 'Something's got to be done about it, Zakr, and we can't wait until you build a new hospital. Although that ought to be started as soon as possible.'

A pained look crossed his face. 'Bethany, why do you always disobey me? I told you I didn't want you there,' he added in weary exasperation.

She kissed him in persuasive appeasement. 'I don't always disobey you. Only when it's absolutely necessary,' she explained. 'And you know perfectly well that you would have visited the wounded if you were well enough, Zakr. It was my duty to do so in your place. It was only right.'

He heaved a long sigh and rolled his eyes at her, but there was no anger in them. Bethany rather suspected that the gleam she saw was one of pride in her, though he would probably never admit it. She was beginning to know him rather well.

He drew her down beside him. 'No more,' he commanded. 'I accept that you've done my duty, but you're not to go again. That is my will, Bethany.'

'I thought you'd say that, Zakr, so I've got this plan...'

He groaned, and his arms tightened around her.

'Are you in pain again?' she asked anxiously.

'Terrible...'

'I'll get you some codeine tablets.'

She started to rise, but his arm snaked around her waist pinning her close to him.

'I think if you kiss me again I will feel a lot better,' he suggested, and the glint of teasing wickedness in his eyes belied any pain at all.

'You fraud! You know you're not allowed to become excited,' she chided, but she kissed him, and for several very satisfying moments Bethany gave in to the pleasure of tasting the passion that rose so quickly between them.

'No more,' she breathed raggedly as she pulled away. 'You'll hurt yourself, Zakr. Dr Hong said you had to have a period of masterly inactivity.'

'Mmmh...the good doctor was undoubtedly talking about out-of-bed activities. I feel so much more alive when I touch you,' he murmured, lifting his hand to her breasts and slowly caressing their firm roundness.

'Zakr...' Bethany was finding it increasingly difficult to concentrate. She hoped he was right about Dr Hong's advice. On the other hand, she shouldn't let him take any unnecessary risks. 'Zakr, I've got to talk to you about my plan,' she forced out, but the husky distractedness in her voice wasn't at all convincing.

He smiled. 'I also have a plan.'

'Zakr...' she pleaded, trying to force his hand away.

Her attempt at resistance grew more and more ineffectual. Zakr rolled his body on to hers and they made love, quickly and fiercely, driven by a hunger for each other that could no longer be controlled.

However, guilt swiftly agitated Bethany out of her deep satisfaction. 'Did you hurt yourself?' she asked anxiously.

Zakr laughed, and the smug grin he wore from ear to ear settled her agitation beyond question.

She smiled her own sweet contentment. 'Well, now will you listen to my plan?' she pressed, completely unabashed about taking advantage of his pleasure in her.

His grin turned rueful. 'Bethany, you have a way of making plans that take you away from me.'

'Not this one, I promise you. Please listen to me.'

'It seems I have no choice,' he said in mock resignation.

'It's about the hospital,' she hurried on. 'Remember you said how difficult it was to get good medical staff who would train your people? Well, I know someone who'd get things shipshape in no time at all. If you give Matron Vaughan the authority, Zakr, she'll do just the right job for you.'

'Matron Vaughan?' He frowned. 'She is not a doctor?'

'No, but she can run a hospital as it should be run. There's no one better, Zakr. Of course, you'll have to offer her a very good salary, because she's the best. And I thought we could give her quarters in the palace until the new hospital is built. If I write to her straight away, she might be able to arrange things so she could come in a couple of months. And Zakr...'

He raised a quizzical eyebrow at her pause. 'There is more?'

'Zakr...' the huge blue eyes filled with luminous appeal '...if I am going to have a baby, I want Matron Vaughan here to... well, just to be here.'

'Then so it shall be,' he said softly. He picked up her hand and threaded his fingers through hers, squeezing possessively. 'We will have a son, Bethany. I know it.'

She shook her head at him. 'Zakr, you can't possibly know that.'

His eyes twinkled indulgently. 'Did I not know that you would come to love me?'

Bethany didn't bother to point out that their relationship had not exactly been smooth-going, and if it hadn't been for the threat of an international incident...on the other hand, had there really been a threat?

Bethany remembered the tracking device Zakr had put on her jeep. He could be very tricky about some things. Maybe he had seen a short-cut to persuading her into becoming his wife...safeguarding his son and heir. Not that it mattered now. If there had been a threat, it had certainly been defused by their marriage, which had created quite a stir in the media.

'Did you always intend to marry me, Zakr?' she asked, needing to have her curiosity satisfied.

The twinkle warmed into a loving caress. 'When I first saw you, Bethany, I sensed the will of Allah...a strange feeling that was entirely new to me...like a touch on my heart. So I appointed Abdul to take care of you, hoping eventually you would be ready to come to me.'

'Why should I do that?' she questioned.

'Because you hungered for me as I hungered for you. It flashed between us the day that the gyr-falcon brought us together. I knew then that whatever had happened to your father, you would be mine.'

The half-smile curved his lips. 'But I did not anticipate your giving me quite so much trouble, Bethany Lyon McGregor. You were so wilful. I had to use every power I could wield in order to bind you to me. And even then you were very difficult.'

Bethany mused over Zakr's reply with a growing sense of satisfaction. He had certainly used all his power of authority...the power of loving...even the emotional power of having a child. There was no doubt about it. Zakr had meant to have her by hook or by crook.

'So you weren't ever going to let me go?' she said, more as an afterthought than a question.

The deep gleam of possessiveness in his eyes emphasised the truth of his answer. 'No. Never.'

Bethany shook her head at him in mock reproval. 'You really are a devil, Zakr.'

He grinned. 'A devil who loves you, my Bethany.'

'Mmmh,' she said consideringly, her eyes sparkling with happiness. 'For that, I can forgive you a lot.'

'Is there something you cannot forgive?'

He tried to look worried.

Bethany thought about it for a while, and decided she was content with her lot in every way, but she wasn't going to tell him that. 'You have too many advantages already, Zakr. I cannot give you any more,' she said archly.

He laughed and bent over her. Bethany languorously stretched her hands above her head and relaxed. She adored it when Zakr made love to her like this, kissing and caressing her face and body at a leisurely pace, arousing so much delicious sensitivity that all she could focus on was what he was doing to her. Mind-stopping, heart-tingling pleasure.

She closed her eyes. 'I didn't want to leave you, Zakr. But the falcon did frighten me,' she confessed.

'In what way?' he murmured, his lips pressing gentle kisses on her eyelids.

'I thought I would be like her, moving only at your command.'

'Mmmh...sometimes I would like that, but I don't think somehow it will happen.'

He started kissing her breasts. 'What...do you mean?' she gasped.

'I love you for the strength of your mind, for your dedication to a cause...you will do what you think is right. And I love the softness of your exquisite body. I love you...love you...'

Her thighs quivered uncontrollably as Zakr's hand trailed softly up the insides of her legs. She skimmed her fingertips over his shoulders and down his back, and smiled as he shuddered with pleasure.

He heaved himself up to look down at her, and caught the lingering end of her smile. His eyes adored her. 'I'll never stop loving you...'

'Kiss me,' she commanded huskily.

'And your will is my will,' he murmured as he bowed his head to obey.

CHAPTER TWELVE

'HE SHALL be named Sayyid Zayn Sadiq,' Zakr declared proudly, his besotted gaze doting on his one-day-old baby son.

Sayyid Zayn *McGregor* Sadiq, Bethany thought to herself, but decided that now was not the time to press that point on her husband. She would have to explain her own family tradition of giving the mother's maiden surname to the firstborn. She gazed adoringly at the baby who was nestled so contentedly against her breast. He was very much Zakr's son, but he did have the McGregor eyes.

'It is as well he is my son,' Zakr observed with a sudden look of hungry desire at Bethany. 'And even of him I am jealous when I see him at your breast, my love.'

His fingers softly stroked her milk-swollen flesh, and Bethany felt the same urgent hunger rise in her. 'Zakr, you'll just have to be patient,' she chided him softly.

He picked up her hand and kissed her fingers. 'I miss you. Our bed is lonely without you. I think I should not have built this hospital. How long do you have to stay here?'

'Only three or four more days. And after all, you do have the heir you wanted,' she reminded him with an indulgent smile.

'It was the will of Allah,' he said smugly.

Bethany laughed. 'I think your will might have had something to do with it. You were right all along, Zakr. I must have got pregnant that first night. It's only just nine months since you took me to your hunting lodge.'

'Ah, yes!' His eyes danced their delight in her. 'That night will live in my memory for ever. You are the most marvellous woman, my Bethany. Did I not always know it?' His gaze dropped proudly to the baby, who burped his satisfaction. 'The mother of my son.'

'Our son,' Bethany corrected him gently.

'Naturally,' he said, unabashed. 'I could not have made such a magnificent child without you. He is perfection.'

Bethany thought so, too. She held him up to her shoulder to pat his back in case he needed to bring up more wind, but he only gave a little baby sigh and went to sleep.

There was a light tap on the door, and Douglas MacArthur McGregor poked his head inside the private maternity-ward room. 'May I come in.'

'Daddy!' Bethany squealed in excitement. 'Come and see your grandson.'

He needed no second invitation, and Zakr, who was no longer jealous of Bethany's love for her father, took enormous pleasure in showing off his son.

Douglas McGregor beamed his love at all three of them. Any man who cherished his daughter as Zakr did commanded his liking and support, and he had very happily agreed to become chancellor of the new university that the sheikh was having built. He was more than content to make his home here with Bethany, in between field trips.

The origin of the Shihuh tribe was still a fascinating puzzle to him. The tribal elders kept using historical terms of reference that he couldn't place with any degree of certainty—the Age of Innocence, the Age of the Great Famine, the Age of the Final Retreat—and while it was all of absorbing interest, his study could wait a while.

After all, a man didn't become a grandfather every day. And his beautiful, clever daughter had certainly done him proud with such a fine baby boy. Definitely royal, he thought smugly. Of course, they would have to add McGregor to that name Zakr had chosen, but he was quite sure Bethany would see to that. Remarkable woman, his daughter!

Another knock on the door announced Matron Vaughan's entrance. She sailed in with two excited little girls in tow. As soon as they saw the baby in Bethany's arms, Fatima and Attiat broke loose and rushed over to the bed to examine their new brother.

'Oh! He's got black hair,' Fatima said in a tone of disappointment.

Bethany smiled. 'Just like you, Fatima. And your father. And your sister. I think black hair is beautiful.'

'But Beth'ny,' Attiat chimed in. 'Can't we have a brother with your hair?'

'Maybe next time.' Bethany's eyes danced teasingly at Zakr. 'If your father wills it.'

'Papa . . .' Fatima faced her father with grave respect. 'Attiat and I think that Bethany's hair is beautiful.'

Zakr picked his daughters up, one in either arm, his expression one of paternal benevolence. 'It would be ungrateful to ask too much from Allah, my children. Very few are granted such glory.' His eyes twinkled at Bethany. 'Besides, perhaps it would not look quite so beautiful on a boy.'

'Come and look at his tiny hands,' Bethany invited. The two girls slithered down and raced back to the bed. 'You see? If you put your finger here, he clutches it.'

They both tried and giggled when the tiny fingers closed around theirs. Their baby brother opened his eyes and blew a bubble, which sent them into paroxysms of laughter.

Matron Vaughan eventually intervened. 'Now, we mustn't get him too excited, must we? Nor spoilt with all this attention,' she declared archly. 'He's already got a will of his own, this one.'

Bethany and Zakr exchanged a knowing look and laughed.

'Time for a nappy-change,' Matron declared, lifting him out of Bethany's arms and laying him carefully in the carry-cot.

'May we come and watch, Matron?' Fatima asked.

The two girls were granted an approving smile. 'Certainly. Never too young to start training.'

'What are you doing away from administration, Matron?' Bethany asked.

The chief executive of the Bethany Lyon McGregor Hospital shot a benevolent look at the sheikh. 'Prince Zakr gave me the authority to do as I please, and I'm pleasing myself. After all, a prince is not an everyday occurrence in our maternity-ward.'

She wheeled the baby off, accompanied by two fascinated little girls who were already determined to become nurses like Bethany. Both of them thought the sun shone out of their stepmother, and not only because of her vividly coloured hair. Bethany had *saved* their father—a story they never tired of hearing—and there was no other woman in the world quite like her. Their father had told them so, and they believed him implicitly.

Douglas McGregor took his leave at the same time, saying he was off to celebrate the occasion with P.J. Weatherly.

Bethany wondered who had smuggled in the illegal bottle of whisky this time, but she just smiled to herself and made no comment.

Zakr locked the door after them.

'I really can't, darling,' she sighed, as he stretched out on the bed with her.

'I know,' he answered softly. 'I just want to hold you and kiss you.'

She curled her arms around his neck and allowed herself to be kissed to the point where she had to kiss him back. 'Oh, I do so love you, Zakr,' she breathed ecstatically.

'I think we will have more sons,' he said. 'But not yet. You are a very beautiful mother, Bethany, but I need you even more as my wife.'

'I'll always be that, Zakr,' she whispered.

The thought came to her that it would never matter how many exotic belly-dancers her husband watched—not that he had bothered with such entertainment since the night before they had married—Bethany knew with absolute certainty that she was the only woman he wanted.

And the want and the need and the love that bound them together was strong enough to bridge two cultures...stronger than the sharpest difference that could ever slice between them. It was the strongest power in the world.

Six exciting series for you every month... from Harlequin

Harlequin Romance·
The series that started it all

Tender, captivating and heartwarming...
love stories that sweep you off to faraway places
and delight you with the magic of love.

◆

Harlequin Presents·
Powerful contemporary love stories...as individual as the women who read them

The No. 1 romance series...
exciting love stories for you, the woman of today...
a rare blend of passion and dramatic realism.

◆

Harlequin Superromance®
It's more than romance... it's Harlequin Superromance

A sophisticated, contemporary romance-fiction
series, providing you with a longer,
more involving read...a richer mix of complex plots,
realism and adventure.

Harlequin American Romance™
Harlequin celebrates the American woman...

...by offering you romance stories written about American women, by American women for American women. This series offers you contemporary romances uniquely North American in flavor and appeal.

◆

Harlequin Temptation™
Passionate stories for today's woman

An exciting series of sensual, mature stories of love...dilemmas, choices, resolutions... all contemporary issues dealt with in a true-to-life fashion by some of your favorite authors.

◆

Harlequin Intrigue™
Because romance can be quite an adventure

Harlequin Intrigue, an innovative series that blends the romance you expect... with the unexpected. Each story has an added element of intrigue that provides a new twist to the Harlequin tradition of romance excellence.

Harlequin Books·

PROD-A-2